B B C

DOCTOR WHO

Shroud of Sorrow

Also available from Broadway:

Plague of the Cypermen *by Justin Richards*

The Dalek Generation *by Nicholas Briggs*

BBC

DOCTOR WHO

Shroud of Sorrow

TOMMY DONBAVAND

Broadway Paperbacks
New York

Published in the United States by Broadway Paperbacks,
an imprint of the Crown Publishing Group,
a division of Random House, Inc., New York.
www.crownpublishing.com

Broadway Paperbacks and its logo, a letter B bisected on the diagonal,
are trademarks of Random House, Inc.

This edition published by arrangement with BBC Books, an imprint of
Ebury Publishing, a division of the Random House Group Limited, London.

Doctor Who is a BBC Wales production for BBC One.
Executive producers: Steven Moffat and Caroline Skinner.

BBC, DOCTOR WHO, and TARDIS (word marks, logos, and devices) are
trademarks of the British Broadcasting Corporation and are used under license.
Cybermen originally created by Kit Pedler and Gerry Davis.

Library of Congress Cataloging-in-Publication Data is available upon request.

ISBN 978-0-385-34678-8
eISBN 978-0-385-34679-5

Printed in the United States of America

Editorial director: Albert DePetrillo
Series consultant: Justin Richards
Project editor: Steve Tribe
Cover design: Lee Binding © Woodlands Books Ltd. 2013
Production: Alex Goddard

1 3 5 7 9 10 8 6 4 2

First Edition

For Arran and Sam,
who watch the Doctor's adventures with me

23 November 1963

PC Reg Cranfield turned the corner into Totter's Lane, the beam of his torch slicing through the fog. It was a thick one tonight, what his dad would have referred to as a 'real pea souper', had he still been alive to say it.

It was a cold one, too. Reg pulled his jacket tighter around himself, hoping that the lads back at the station would remember to keep the teapot warm this time. He didn't want to come back to a cold brew on a night like this. Still, at least the streets were quiet tonight. Everyone was indoors watching the news reports coming in from America. Nasty business, that.

This wasn't his regular beat. He'd swapped shifts at the last minute with his drinking buddy, PC Rawlings, who claimed he was coming down with the flu. Reg wasn't convinced. Fred was as healthy as a horse; he'd never had so much as a sniffle in all the time they'd known each other. Sergeant Clough reckoned it all had something to do with what had happened last night, when Fred had returned to the nick as white as a sheet, blabbering on about 'people in the mist who weren't really there'. More likely he'd stopped off for one too many bracers at the Rose and Crown, but Fred had swapped with him plenty of times over the past few months so he could go and visit his dad.

Reg found himself thinking about his father again. It was two weeks now. Two weeks since he'd slipped away, less than half an hour after Reg had left the old folks' home after his nightly visit. It was almost as though his dad had deliberately held off dying until his only son was safely on the number 91 bus back home before heading for the pearly gates.

Not that his dad had believed in any form of life after death. In fact, he only went to church on Christmas Eve because he'd promised Reg's mother that he would continue to do so after she had died. 'If there was an afterlife, I'd know about it,' he used to tease. 'Your mother never stopped nagging me when she was alive, and there'd be no stopping her coming back from beyond the grave to do the same.'

Of course, now his dad had gone off to join his mum. Wherever that was.

Reg hadn't even found out until he telephoned

the home from the station the next morning to see if his dad had had a comfortable night. He didn't have a telephone at his flat, so the staff at the home had no way of contacting him. Of course, now there was no point in getting a line installed at all.

His torch swept across the wooden gates of Foreman's scrapyard, and Reg paused to check they were securely locked. There had been rumours of teenagers hanging around the gates at all hours of the day and night, although no break-ins had been reported, and nothing had gone missing. Still that didn't mean the yard was going to become a hang-out for school kids when they should be at home with their families. Not on his watch.

'Reggie…'

Reg spun round, waving his torch to and fro like a fencer's foil. 'Who's there?'

'Reggie!'

Reg shivered. This wasn't funny. The only person who ever called him by that name was his dad. Whoever was doing so now would have some serious explaining to do.

'I said, who's there?'

Then his torch picked out a face. A face looming slowly out of the thick mist. A face that didn't seem to be connected to anything else.

'This is Police Constable Cranfield,' he announced. 'Identify yourself!'

'Reggie – it's me!'

Reg felt his legs turn to jelly, forcing him to press his free hand against the scrap yard gates to steady himself. 'Dad?'

The face was clearer now, taking shape as more wisps of fog blew in on the breeze. It was, without a shadow of a doubt, Reg's father.

'Dad!' he croaked, his mouth suddenly bone dry. 'Dad, I... I don't...'

'You left me, Reggie.'

'What?'

'You left me that night. Left me to die alone.'

Reg's legs gave way and he slumped back against the gate, rattling the padlocked chain. 'No... You don't understand!'

'I was alone, Reggie. Alone and in pain. I couldn't even call for help.'

'B-but, Dad...,' said Reg, blinking back tears. 'I had to get the last bus. You know I always get that bus when I come to see... when I *came* to see you. You know that.'

The face was drifting closer now, swelling out of the fog, growing more and more real with every passing second.

'You don't know what it's like, Reggie,' the face said, its expression twisting into an angry sneer. 'To be abandoned by your family. To be left alone by those you've cared for all your life!'

'It wasn't like that!' sobbed Reg, the tears flowing freely now. 'If I'd known, I'd have stayed. I promise!'

'Stayed to watch me die?'

'Yes. N-no! I mean I would have stayed there so I could have got help for you!'

'But you didn't stay, Reggie. After all I've done for you!'

'Dad, please...' Reg's voice was little more than a whisper.

The face darted forward towards him, mouth wide and teeth bared. Reg dropped his torch to the ground and covered his eyes with his hands. 'No! NO!'

Then the face of PC Reg Cranfield's dead father began to scream.

Chapter 1

The TARDIS engines groaned like a weary pensioner as the blue box slowly climbed – an inch at a time – above a vast maelstrom of churning water. Huge waves smashed into each other as the storm grew in strength, spraying up showers of pale green bubbles that splashed through the open doors into the entrance of the control room – and smelled vaguely of avocado.

In the midst of all this water and foam was a chain. A big, thick, strong chain. One end was wrapped around the bottom of the console, from where it stretched as taut as a tightrope out through the doors and down into the fragrant surf below. The metal links creaked in protest as the TARDIS rose a little higher, finally taking the full weight of what was connected to the other end.

'Anything?' called the Doctor. He was soaking wet and covered from head to toe in soap suds, and had wedged his feet against the base of the console for grip. His knuckles whitened as he pulled back on a blue-handled lever, urging the ship to ascend even higher.

Gripping tightly to the telephone behind one of the TARDIS doors, Clara cautiously leaned out over the water and risked a glance down at the chain as it disappeared into the frothy, emerald storm below them. 'Nothing yet!' she shouted back, water dripping from her hair and into her eyes. She risked letting go of the door with one hand to wipe them.

The TARDIS was now flying at close to a 45-degree angle. One slip and the Doctor knew he would follow the chain out of the door and down into the water before he could say 'Alfava Metraxis'. Spinning a wheel on the next console panel around, he reached out with his free hand and flicked a series of switches, grinding the already screaming engines up a gear. 'Come on, sexy!' he urged. 'I know you can do it!'

'Thanks for the compliment,' said Clara. 'I didn't know you cared.'

His cheeks flushing, the Doctor released the switches long enough to tenderly pat the console. 'Sorry, dear,' he whispered. 'I meant you – not her. Honest.'

Once again the chain creaked under the weight of its burden. The Doctor eyed it warily, briefly wondering whether he'd chosen a strong enough metal for the task at hand. He kept a chain made from a dwarf star alloy on hand for really big jobs – but it would have taken at least ten of him to carry it up from the store room, and he hadn't had time to make the telephone calls to arrange that.

'There!' cried Clara. 'I can see the ship. It's almost at the surface.'

'Good!' the Doctor shouted. 'Let's go for one... last... pull!' Gritting his teeth, he slammed another lever down, re-routing even more power to the ship's engines. 'Well, that's everything in the freezer room defrosting now...'

The chain clunked loudly as another metal link slid over the doorstep, splintering the wood and causing Clara to hold on tighter than ever. She flicked her long, dark hair out of her eyes, spattering the TARDIS doors with a mixture of mud and bubbles. The mess almost seemed to form the shape of a face. She stared at it for a moment. It looked almost like...

The TARDIS lurched and Clara fell back against the door, obliterating the pattern with her shoulder. She looked down again. Beneath her feet, an ocean of scented waves heaved and boiled. It was bizarre to think that, less than thirty minutes ago, she had been kneeling down there in what was hard, baked earth.

Suddenly, a voice crackled through the console speakers. 'Doctor! Are you there? It's Penny...'

The Doctor made to flick the switch that would activate the microphone – then realised that both of his hands were busy holding the TARDIS in position. With a sigh, he leaned forward and forced the switch to the 'on' position with his chin.

'Hellllloooo Penny! This is the Doctor, reading you loud and clear. How are you?'

'All present and correct, thankfully,' came the reply. 'We made it back on board the *Carter* just before the flood hit us. Had to leave a lot of our equipment behind, though.'

'Equipment can be replaced,' said the Doctor. 'People can't. Well, there is one planet where they can, but I'm not allowed back there. Long story. Tried to get a refund on a shop-soiled Australian flight attendant without her permission.'

Then, with a sudden lurch backwards, the TARDIS righted itself and the chain went slack.

'We did it!' squealed Clara. 'They're out!'

The Doctor pushed the levers back into position, then raced to join his companion. There, rising free of the water to hover outside the doorway, was the class 2 exploration cruiser, the SS *Howard Carter*. It was a small ship, designed more for short-range planet hopping than interstellar flight. Its three-man crew waved their grateful thanks from behind the tinted windows of the cockpit.

Professor Penelope Holroyde spoke into her headset, her voice still echoing out from the console speaker. 'You saved our lives, Doctor,' she said. 'How can we ever begin to thank you?'

'No thanks necessary,' replied the Doctor. 'We do this sort of thing all the time.'

'Just a normal day at the office for us,' laughed Clara.

'Well, you have one grateful archaeological team right here,' said Penny.

'How's the ship?' asked the Doctor.

Professor Holroyde checked with her co-pilot before replying. 'The water's temporarily knocked out one of our engines, but we should be able to get it started again.'

The Doctor smiled. 'That's good to hear.'

'Have a safe journey,' called Clara.

'We will, thanks to you,' said Penny. 'Releasing your grappling hook now…'

There was a *clunk*, and the pincers on the front of the *Carter* released the thick chain. The Doctor whipped out his sonic screwdriver and fired a blast over his shoulder. A switch spun on the console, and the chain began to reel itself back inside the TARDIS.

Free of the lifeline, the SS *Howard Carter* turned lazily in the air and ignited its one remaining booster, disappearing into the clouds of fine mist spat up by the stormy sea. The Doctor and Clara stood in the doorway, waving, until the ship was lost from view

– then they slammed the TARDIS doors shut, and turned to glare at one another.

'That,' barked the Doctor, 'was all your fault!' He tore off his sopping wet coat and tossed it over his shoulder, then stomped back to the console, squelching all the way.

Clara followed close behind. 'What do you mean, my fault?'

The Doctor furiously typed coordinates into the console keyboard. 'I was really enjoying myself down there. But oh no – you had to go and ruin it!'

'*I* ruined it?'

'Yes,' snapped the Doctor without looking up. 'You ruined it – and you made my bow tie soggy!'

'At least you're clean,' said Clara. 'Half an hour ago you were completely covered in dirt. We both were.'

'It's called archaeology,' said the Doctor, spinning to face her. 'You're *supposed* to get dirty. It's part of the fun.'

'Well, it didn't feel like fun to me!'

'And you made sure we all knew that, didn't you?' The Doctor raised his hands, opening and closing his fingers as though operating a pair of puppets.

'Oh, Doctor! I'm so bored, and my jeans are getting all muddy!' one hand said, the Doctor mimicking Clara's voice. 'Boo hoo hoo!'

'Well, why don't you go back to the TARDIS until we're finished?' the other 'Doctor' hand said.

'No,' replied the 'Clara' hand, 'because you'll lose all track of time like you always do and keep on having lots of fun without me.'

Clara glared at the Doctor's hands. 'Is one of those supposed to be me?'

The Doctor raised his left hand. 'That one.'

'So the other one's you?'

'Yes.'

'The chin's too small,' said Clara, skipping down the steps at the back of the room and starting to strip out of her wet clothes.

The Doctor glanced from one hand to the other, then dropped them down to his sides. 'You still didn't have to spoil everything,' he muttered, quickly turning his back when he realised that Clara was changing. 'Can't you do that in the TARDIS wardrobe?'

'No, I can't,' said Clara. 'It was your idea to keep a spare set of clothes in the console room for emergencies, remember? Besides, if I go wandering off to the wardrobe, I might ruin something else for you on the way.'

'There's no need to be sarcastic,' said the Doctor, pulling a sulky face. He threw back the flight lever and, with a far less laboured wheeze than before, the central column began to rise and fall. 'Sarcasm is the lowest form of wit, you know – although I once met a Sontaran stand-up comedian who could challenge it for the record.'

'I still don't get what I did wrong,' said Clara. 'All I did was press a few buttons.'

'Exactly!'

'But I didn't know they'd drained an entire sea for the dig, did I?'

The Doctor swept his wet hair back from his eyes, then sniffed at his fingers. 'Gosh,' he smiled. 'I smell faintly fruity!' His stern expression fell back into place. 'Why do you think the area of Venofax we were digging in is called Ocean Peninsula?'

'I dunno,' Clara shrugged. 'I figured it was named after whoever first found it. Dave Ocean, maybe?'

'*Dave* Ocean?' said the Doctor, arching an eyebrow.

'Well, how should I know? You didn't tell me I was sitting next to the controls for the floodgates!'

'I didn't think I'd have to,' said the Doctor, flitting from one side of the console to another and spinning a dial. 'I didn't think you'd start pressing buttons, willy nilly.'

'I was looking for a water dispenser.'

'Well, you certainly found one of those.'

'All right,' Clara sighed. 'So I pressed the wrong buttons – but what's with all the bubbles, and the whole sea stinking of avocado?'

'That's the point!' the Doctor cried, changing sides once more to adjust a dial. 'No one knows! The Venofaxons are extinct. That's why Professor Holroyde and her team spent several months and a lot of money draining the sea so they could excavate beneath it and find out what was going on. And then you came along…'

Now in dry clothes, Clara climbed back up to the console level and dropped into the seat beside the steps, arms folded. For a moment neither of them spoke. The only sound was the rasping hum of the engines and the occasional flick of a switch as the Doctor fiddled with the settings. Satisfied everything was running smoothly, he grabbed his spare jacket from the opposite seat and disappeared up to the walkway above.

'That's why I wanted to get involved in the first place,' he called back into the control room. 'Think about it. An entire world covered in a bubble-bath sea. It's fascinating! All we had to do was find a planet populated by thirty-foot rubber ducks and get them together.'

Despite her mood, Clara laughed. 'Don't forget the giant sponge!' she said. 'I reckon we'll need one the size of a blue whale.'

The Doctor reappeared, dry as a bone, and smiled at Clara – but his expression quickly fell. 'What's the matter now?' he asked. 'I thought we were getting back to normal.'

'We are,' said Clara. 'Well, as normal as this place gets.'

'Then why are you crying?'

'What?' Clara touched her cheeks with her

fingers. They were wet with tears. 'I don't know. Why am I crying?'

Suddenly, there was an explosion of sparks from the console. The Doctor jumped up and wafted away the resulting plume of smoke.

'What's wrong?' asked Clara, racing to his side.

'I have absolutely no idea,' said the Doctor. 'Wait – yes I have.' He wiped his hand across the surface of the console. It came away wet. 'I think… I think the TARDIS is crying as well.'

'That's ridiculous,' scoffed Clara. 'It's just bubble-bath water. It must have splashed up there when you rewound the chain.'

The Doctor licked his fingertips. 'No,' he said. 'That was avocado. This is salty – like tears.' He thought for a second, then spun on Clara. 'Did you say something cruel to the TARDIS while I was getting changed?'

'No! Of course not.'

'Did you call her fat?'

'What?'

'Because she's not fat. She's just bigger on the inside.'

'You're crazy. You know that, don't you?'

'Well, she can't be crying for no reason.'

'Why not?' demanded Clara. 'I'm crying as well – but you're not asking her if she called *me* chubby.'

Another shower of sparks sent them both ducking beneath the console for cover. When the Doctor re-emerged, he found the readout in front of him skipping backwards and forwards at an alarming rate. 'No, no, no, NO!' He sprang to his feet and began to work feverishly at the controls.

'What's the matter?' asked Clara, peeking over the edge of the console.

'The TARDIS's tears are shorting out the helmic regulator.'

'They're *not* tears! It's probably just condensation or something.'

'Whatever it is, it's pulling us off course.' The Doctor used his sleeve to dry the console, but it made little difference. 'Aha!' he cried, noticing the scarf around Clara's neck. He snatched it to finish the job.

'Hey!' she cried.

'That's for the soggy bow tie.'

Then the floor jolted with a familiar *boom*, and the console fell silent.

'We've landed,' said the Doctor.

'Where?' asked Clara. 'When?'

'I'm not sure…' The Doctor scurried round to the monitor screen. The display hissed back at him, a grey mass of static. Then, faintly at first, a face began to form out of random particles in the centre of the screen. A face he hadn't seen for a very long time.

'Astrid!'

'Astrid?' repeated Clara, hurrying over. 'What's an Astrid when it's at home?'

The Doctor quickly flicked off the display, pausing for a split second to gather his thoughts. 'It's nothing,' he said, turning away from the monitor. 'The time circuits have gone wobbly, that's all. They won't be able to give us an accurate reading until I can repair them. Until then – there's only one way to find out where and when we are…'

He bounded down the stairs and flung open the door. 'Marvellous! It's a hospital,' he cried. 'Just the place for a Doctor.'

Clara stepped out of the TARDIS and closed the door behind her. She smiled to a young woman hurrying past clutching a bouquet of flowers. 'They're pretty,' she said. 'I bet they're going to really brighten up someone's day.'

The woman glared back as if she'd been insulted, then scuttled away, eyes fixed to the ground.

'Nice to meet you, too,' Clara called after her. 'Doctor…'

But the Doctor was already striding away down the corridor, and Clara was forced to dodge past a sniffling nurse in order to catch up with him. 'Look,' she said, pointing to a commemorative plaque on the wall behind the nurse's station. '"Welcome to Parkland Memorial Hospital". I've heard of this place somewhere before.'

'Really?' said the Doctor. 'Where?'

'I can't remember,' said Clara as a sullen porter

approached them, pushing an equally glum patient in a wheelchair. 'Although I doubt it was because it had won a "cheeriest hospital of the year" award.'

The Doctor held up his hand to stop the porter and bent to greet the occupant of the wheelchair. 'Hello,' he said. 'I'm the Doctor. How are you today?'

'I've felt better,' grumbled the old man. 'We all have.'

'Yes, well I expect that's why you're in a hospital. Can I ask which city we're in?'

The old man looked up at him suspiciously. 'Which city?'

'Yes. It's er… a cognitive reasoning test. You know, just to make sure you aren't loopy or anything. And even if you are, no matter. Some of the best people I know are, you know… a little bit sideways. Take Isambard Kingdom Brunel, for example. Mad as a box of frogs. He only built all those bridges because he was afraid of walking at ground level. Claimed pixies were biting his ankles.'

The porter scowled. 'Are you sure you're a doctor?'

'Quite sure!' beamed the Doctor. 'In fact…' He rummaged through his jacket pockets and produced a stethoscope, which he hung round his neck. 'There, see!'

'So what's wrong with me, then?' demanded the old man.

The Doctor whipped out his sonic screwdriver

and ran a quick diagnostic scan over the man's body. 'Kidney stones,' he pronounced, examining the results. 'Drink plenty of fluids and you'll be right as rain in a few days' time.'

'Nothing serious, then,' said Clara, bending to offer the man her widest grin. 'Can you tell us which city we're in, now?'

'You people make me sick!' barked the old man. He turned to the porter. 'Get me out of here!'

'Have I got spinach in my teeth, or something?' Clara demanded.

The Doctor snatched a newspaper from the porter's back pocket as the patient was wheeled away. 'If only it were that easy to brush off,' he said, studying the front page.

'Well, something's made this lot go out and buy a one-way ticket to Grumpsville!'

'I think it might be this,' the Doctor said, handing over the newspaper. It was the *Dallas Morning News*.

The front page displayed a photograph of a man Clara remembered from her school history lessons, with a single bold headline above. She read it aloud. '"Kennedy Slain on Dallas Street".' She gasped. 'But that means…'

'Yes,' said the Doctor, indicating the date at the top of the page. 'It's 23 November 1963. We're in Dallas, Texas – the day after the assassination of President John F. Kennedy.'

Chapter 2

Mae Callon pushed the pile of paperwork to one side, folded her arms on her desk and rested her head down in one last attempt at sleep. It had been a long night – the longest she could remember in her five years working at the *Morning News*. A night she would never forget, no matter how hard she tried. But, like before, sleep wouldn't come.

The images and sounds assaulted her, just as they had every time she had closed her eyes since yesterday. The bright sunlight streaming down over Dealey Plaza as people cheerfully awaited their first sight of the motorcade. President Kennedy, his wife and Governor Connolly waving to the crowds. Mae herself, standing on tiptoe to get a better view of the President – her pencil scratching over the surface of her notepad. Then a flash – far off to the right, and high up. Seeming to come from the School Book Depository. A crack – like that of a whip. Then another flash. And another. And the screams. Dear God, the screams.

Mae forced herself to sit up and open her eyes. She hadn't seen the bullets hit the President or Governor Connolly herself – there were too many people crowded in front of her – but she'd spoken to many people who had. The things they had described were horrific. Things she'd had to transcribe for her report in the morning edition. Now they were seared into her mind just as if she had witnessed them herself, and she wasn't alone in her grief. From around the office came the sound of sobbing as the full impact of yesterday's events hit home.

She slid her chair back. If she wasn't going to sleep, she might as well work. There was an article to write on Lyndon B. Johnson's first twenty-four hours as President and if she was going to tackle it without sleep, that meant coffee. She crossed the office, trying to avoid looking at Kennedy staring up from the front page of the paper – a copy of which sat on each of her fellow reporters' desks. Perhaps if she didn't look at the picture, the images in her head might subside a little.

Coffee acquired, she made her way back to her desk – skilfully avoiding yet another 'isn't it terrible?' conversation with one of the sub-editors. She placed her coffee onto the same spot she always did, adding yet another ring to several years' worth of stains marking the wood, flipped over her newspaper so Kennedy could no longer look at her, and pulled her typewriter closer.

She'd got as far as typing the title, 'Oath on Aircraft', when a large brown envelope dropped onto her keyboard. 'Forget the Johnson piece,' said her editor, Ben Parsons. 'I'm giving it to Jim.'

Mae glanced up at her boss in surprise. 'Jim?' she queried. 'Doesn't he have enough to do with the sports pages?'

Ben sighed. 'You think anyone's gonna do more than glance at those for the next few days?'

'I guess not.'

'Jim's a good kid,' said Ben. 'He wants to make the move to the news floor. Taking the Johnson story will help.'

'So what's this,' asked Mae, making to open the envelope. Ben rested his hand on hers to stop her.

'This… isn't pleasant,' he said. 'They're stills from cine footage taken by some guy called Zapruder. He was on the opposite side of the street from you yesterday – and he caught everything on film. Everything.'

'What? How did you get hold of them so quickly?'

'*Life* magazine had Kodak do a rush job on developing them,' said Ben. 'They plan to publish them in this week's edition and, so long as we don't steal their scoop, I got permission from a friend there for you to use them as well. He flew them down this morning.'

Mae looked surprised. 'Why me?'

'Look around you,' Ben replied. 'I can't trust any of these hacks not to go to town on these pictures. Make a big, gory deal out of them. But I trust you.'

'That's... very kind,' said Mae.

Ben chuckled. 'I'm not doing it to be kind, Mae. I'm doing it because it's my job. You'll treat these with respect, and that's what people need after a damn mess like this – a little respect. Not some god-awful creep show.'

Mae waited until Ben had left before taking a sip of coffee and opening the envelope. She slid the photographs out upside down, their plain white backs showing first. After a moment or two, she took a deep breath and flipped them over.

They were everything she had dreaded they would be. A genuine, second-by-second record of the murder of President John F. Kennedy. She flipped through the pictures with trembling hands. President Kennedy waving to the crowds. President Kennedy raising his hands to clutch at the front of his throat. Jacqueline Kennedy leaning in to her wounded husband. Then – oh, dear Lord – President Kennedy's head. It just... It...

Mae tossed the photographs aside, her eyes flooding with tears. She reached for her coffee, took a big gulp and was about to put the mug down when something unusual caught her eye. The coffee stain on her desk. She'd never really looked at it closely before. But now she did. Now that it had the newest smudge from her current cup of coffee – the stain made a face. The face of her late grandmother.

Wiping the tears from her eyes, Mae set the coffee aside at the other edge of her desk and studied the stain. The likeness to Grandma Betty was astonishing. The brown smears in the centre of the blemish were just like her eyes – kind, warm and mischievous. And the curved lines at the top, which she knew were nothing more than part rings made by spilled coffee – they formed the curls of her hair. She always had it cut and set the same way, once a month without fail – just like that! And the mouth. The mouth had to be Betty's. Pursed lips, smiling and scolding at exactly the same time. Just as ready to praise as to criticise.

Mae clasped her hand to her mouth and laughed. If she hadn't stopped attending church shortly after Grandma Betty passed away, she'd have called this a miracle. Now, the only name she had for it was… well, she didn't have a name for it, other than weird. She had to get Phil to fetch his camera and come take a shot of—

'Why weren't you there?'

Mae froze. 'Who said that?'

'Who do you think, girl?'

Mae stared at the stain. 'G… Grandma?'

It couldn't be! No – it mustn't be! The face of Grandma Betty on her desk was moving!

'In the hospital, Mae. Why weren't you there? At the end?'

Mae pulled her eyes away from the impossible image and stared around the newsroom, certain that someone would be watching her fall for this sick prank – or whatever it was. But everyone was hard at work. No one was even looking her way.

OK, so it wasn't a prank. It must be the lack of sleep. Yes – that was it. Her mind was starting to play tricks on her. Either that or she was going insane. But what if – just, what if – it was really happening? There was only one way to find out…

She looked back down at her desk. 'I had to go to Washington, Grandma. For the newspaper. Cuba was threatening to launch missiles…'

'You always did put your job before your family!' snapped the stain.

Mae felt her eyes grow wet again. 'I tried to come home, Grandma. When they said you didn't have long. But there was some kind of problem with the radar at Dulles Airport, and everything was backed up. I couldn't get a flight.'

'After all I did for you! Practically raised you after that no-good father of yours upped and left, what with your momma takin' to drink an' all. You left me to die alone on purpose!'

Mae flinched at the allegation. 'What? No, I...'

'Hoped to come home and find yourself with access to Grandma Betty's savings account, huh?'

'No! Grandma, all I ever cared about was you!'

Slowly, the coffee-stain face began to bulge out of the desk – the wood stretching and warping as it took on a three-dimensional shape. The badly varnished grain twisted into the old woman's wrinkled skin, and dark, vacant hollows sank away where her eyes and mouth should have been. And that mouth kept moving, speaking, accusing.

'You never cared one speck for me, Mae Louise Callon. You just wanted my money.'

'No, that's not true!'

The head was almost fully formed now, the writhing shape sending Mae's paperwork tumbling to the floor.

'Grandma Betty,' she sobbed. 'You have to believe me!'

Then the old woman's mouth stretched wide – wider than any human mouth could ever open – and she began to scream.

Mae jumped back, knocking the remainder of her cup of coffee off the desk. Instinct kicked in and she tried to catch the mug, spilling hot coffee on her bare arm, causing her to cry out. She jumped to her feet and grabbed her typewriter with her uninjured hand, slamming it down hard on top of the writhing face.

'No! No! No!' she screamed. Again and again she battered against the vision until, eventually, it shrank back into the desk, nothing more than a coffee stain once more.

By the time she slumped back into her chair, her hand clamped over the red scald on her arm, the entire office had stopped work to stare at her.

Chapter 3

The window from where the sniper had apparently shot President Kennedy was on the sixth floor of the Texas School Book Depository – exactly five more floors than FBI agent Warren Skeet wanted to climb.

He glanced out through the door at the younger, fitter agents scouring Dealey Plaza for clues, evidence that might build a case against the young man the police were holding in custody for committing yesterday's atrocity. Beyond them, on the other side of the cordon, stood a crowd of stunned and crying onlookers, drawn to see the scene of the tragedy for themselves.

Warren knew he could ask to swap with one of the junior agents, use his years of experience to pull rank and get the cushy job pottering about in the sunshine while one of the others searched the sixth floor – but that would mean admitting he was too old and out of shape to climb the stairs. It wouldn't seem like much at first – just a bit of a laugh around the coffee machine – but, sooner or later, he would arrive at work to find an envelope taped to the door of his locker, and his career would be over.

Still, he could put off the climb. He could go for an early lunch down at Don's Bar, where a grilled cheese sandwich and a restorative nip of scotch often did wonders to lighten his mood. There was always the risk that the chief would be in there – that was the downside to frequenting the so-called 'bureau bar' – but, so long as he ate the sandwich quickly, and kept the scotch out of sight, he shouldn't get any grief. Unable to decide, he chose to let the universe make the decision for him and pulled a coin from his pocket. Heads for the scotch, tails for the stairs…

Dammit! He made for the stairs.

Warren had started out as a rookie cop almost forty years ago now. An excellent service record and swift progression up the chain of command meant that it wasn't long before he was noticed and recruited by the Bureau. He'd had a partner in the early days – a guy of almost exactly the same age, yet they couldn't have been more different. Jock had a wife and kids, a happy home life, the works. Warren's own marriage had lasted less than a year, and he had no intention of trying another one on for size. Jock said one saving grace of the break-up was that Warren and Shirley hadn't had kids. There was no one stuck in the middle, no need to stay on barely speaking terms with the woman who had left him for the local butcher, of all damn people. Yeah... No one to call him on his birthday or father's day. No one to give him good reason to keep his apartment clean, or his drinking under control.

Still, what he lacked in his own life, he made up for through Jock. His partner's family welcomed him into their home with open arms. They'd even bought a cot for the basement so that he wouldn't have to drive home after a late-night card game, or if he and Jock had celebrated closing a case with a few beers. Despite his single status, he couldn't remember a time when he'd had to spend a Thanksgiving or Christmas alone. At least, not until that Sunday afternoon at the airport...

Warren reached the third-floor landing and paused for breath – although paused for an almighty coughing fit might have been more accurate. He could feel his heart pounding in his chest, and his shirt was slick against his back with sweat. He'd never been the fittest guy on the team – Jock won out there, as well. And he often wondered if things might have been different if he had taken up jogging instead of spending his weekend on the couch with a six-pack and the game on the wireless.

Word had come in that there was to be a major

meeting of mob bosses – right here on their home turf. Some of the country's biggest gangsters would be flying in to Dallas. For hungry agents like Warren and Jock, it was as though someone had handed them half of the United States' most wanted on a silver platter.

The boys had staked out the airport for two days straight before they spotted their first target. A new-to-the-scene mob boss from New Jersey called Pinky Bradford. He had a couple of goons with him and, judging by the bulges beneath their jackets, they were packing heat. So, the plan was to follow them back to their hotel, then catch them when they were off guard. At least – that's what Warren expected the plan to be.

Jock didn't want to leave the airport in case any of the other names on their list flew in unexpectedly and the collars went to rival agents. So he followed Bradford and his guys out to the taxi rank and tried to arrest them singlehandedly. By the time Warren realised what his partner was doing, it was already too late. He ran, faster than he'd ever run before, at the sound of gunfire – but it still felt like everything was happening in slow motion. By the time he left the terminal building, Jock was down and dying. Warren let off a few rounds and winged one of Bradford's boys – but there was nothing he could do for his partner.

After the funeral, Warren tried to visit Jock's wife

and kids a few times, but the atmosphere quickly turned cold. He knew there was no way they could blame him for Jock's death – he'd had no idea that his friend was planning to act so soon – but they were furious that he hadn't done the right thing and died alongside his partner. Ever since that day, Warren had worked alone and on far less important cases. Gone were the days of apprehending mobsters. Now he spent much of his time chasing down petty crooks and conmen. If it wasn't for the 'all hands on deck' requirement of this investigation, he had no doubt he'd currently be doing the coffee run for his fellow agents.

By the time he reached the sixth floor it had started raining. A couple of the forensic guys were just about finishing up, packing away their equipment. They shared an amused glance at the sight of Warren's flushed face.

'Hey, Skeet! You OK, man? You don't look so good.'

'I'm fine,' Warren barked back. 'You guys finished playing with your make-up brushes yet?'

With barely disguised sneers, the lab guys disappeared, leaving Warren alone. He took a few minutes to allow his ragged breathing to ease, then made for the window supposedly used by the gunman. The whole area was still covered in fingerprint powder so, taking care not to touch anything important, he stepped up to the window and angled himself to get the best view of the plaza below. Jeez, that was a long way off. This guy must have been some shot to—

'Hey, ol' buddy!'

Warren spun round, expecting to find another of the crime-scene guys ready to ridicule him, but he was alone. One of them must have left their police radio up here or something. He turned back to the window – and found Jock staring back at him.

No – it wasn't Jock. It was just the pattern of raindrops on the window pane – but it looked like Jock. Exactly like Jock. And it was moving!

'What's the matter, pal?' said the watery face. 'Nothin' to say to your partner?'

Warren's breath caught in his throat. 'Jock?' he croaked.

'The one and only, big guy!' replied the raindrops. 'I would ask how you've been keepin', but I can pretty much see that for myself.'

Again Warren looked round – half-expecting to see his own rapidly cooling dead body lying at the top of the stairs. But the jackhammer pounding away in his chest told him he was still very much alive. Then it had to be down to one of the other agents. 'OK, very funny guys!' he yelled. 'Whoever's doing this – you're a sick bastard!'

'No one's doin' anything, buddy!' said Jock. 'Least of all you.'

Warren turned back to his dead partner. 'What

do you mean?'

'Where was my back-up, ol' chum? Where were you when the bullets started to fly?'

'I was running to help you!' Warren cried.

'Runnin' my eye!' laughed Jock wickedly. 'The only thing I've ever seen you run is a bar tab. You left me out in the cold, Skeet. You left me to die!'

Warren reached out, pressing the flat of his hand against the inside of the window pane. To hell with the fingerprints. 'You can't blame me for that,' he said. 'I... I wasn't ready. You acted alone!'

'You abandoned me!' roared Jock. The glass in the window began to bulge inwards and Warren leapt back, pulling his hand away as though it had been burned. 'You were supposed to have my back, and you abandoned me!'

'No, no... It wasn't like that!' Warren started to back away, but the face kept on coming, stretching into the building until it resembled a fully formed head.

'And I know exactly why you left me to take the hit,' bellowed Jock. 'All that time you spent at my place with Cathy and the kids – you wanted it for yourself. You had to get me out of the picture so that you could move in on my family!'

Warren could feel tears stinging his eyes. 'How can you say that?' he yelled. 'I would never do that to you. You were my partner! You were my friend!'

The glass face twisted, its raindrop features

running together to form a sneer. 'And *you* were the reason I died!'

'*No!*' Warren snatched up a box of books and hurled it at the face. The box smashed through the window, landing a heavy thump on the ground six storeys below.

Immediately, Warren's radio crackled into life. 'Agent Skeet! Do you require assistance? I repeat, do you require assistance?'

Warren looked out of the shattered window pane at the younger agents staring up at him from below and he unclipped his own radio from his belt. 'Negative,' he replied. 'No assistance required. I, er... I tripped and knocked into a stack of boxes.' He pulled a coin from his pocket and was about to flip it when he stopped, stared at it for a second, then slipped it back into his pocket with a sigh. 'Let's just say it came up tails,' he said to himself. 'I'm going for a long, wet lunch.'

Chapter 4

'Next!'

Mae lifted the wet cloth from the burn mark on her arm just long enough to peek underneath and grimace, then she followed the sound of the voice and entered the doctor's office.

The figure sitting at the desk wasn't exactly what she had expected. His coat was purple, rather than white, for one thing – although he did have a stethoscope draped around his neck. And when he spoke, he sounded British.

'Hello!' he said cheerily. 'I'm the Doctor. And I'm *a* doctor today as well. Quite exciting! This is my friend, Nurse Clara.' He gestured to a girl leaning against the wall at the back of the room, who waved pleasantly. She wasn't dressed as a nurse at all.

'I've, er... scalded my arm,' said Mae. 'The woman in the emergency room sent me down here, but I'm not sure I've come to the right place.'

'Of course you're in the right place,' beamed the Doctor. 'I'm clearly a doctor, and you've got a boo-hoo.' He paused to look over at Clara. 'Would you say "boo-hoo" was the correct word to use in a case like this, nurse?'

'Too early to tell,' Clara replied, 'at least until we've examined the patient. It could just as easily be an "ouchie".'

'Very good point – go straight to the top of the class!' The Doctor spun round in a circle on his chair, stopping to face Mae once more. 'What's your name?'

'Mae. Mae Callon.'

The Doctor's angular face split into a wide smile. 'Now then, Mae Callon. What say we take a look at this burn of yours...'

Carefully, Mae removed the wet cloth to reveal the angry red mark on her left forearm. Clara drew in a sharp breath at the sight of it.

'Now that,' said the Doctor, leaning in to get a better look, 'is most definitely an "ouchie". And have you noticed, Mae, that the shape of the burn looks a little bit like a face?'

The effect was instant. Mae collapsed to the floor, sobbing heavily. The Doctor sat back, eyes wide in alarm as Clara hurried over to wrap her arms around the crying girl.

'You might have a stethoscope,' she hissed, helping Mae up into a chair, 'but your bedside manner sucks!'

The Doctor looked horrified. 'What did I say?' he mouthed.

'I don't know,' said Clara. 'But you've had two of us in tears today already. Three if you include the TARDIS.'

'It's OK,' sniffed Mae, wiping her eyes with her good hand. 'You didn't say anything to upset me. It's just that the face looks exactly like my Grandma Betty.'

The Doctor wheeled his chair noisily over to sit in front of Mae. 'Grandma Betty, eh? And would I be right in thinking that Grandma Betty has passed away?' He braced himself for another bout of tears, but none came. Mae simply nodded.

'How did you know that?' asked Clara.

'Call it a lucky guess,' replied the Doctor. He pulled out a strange-looking piece of medical equipment and took hold of Mae's left wrist. 'May I?'

Mae nodded again. The Doctor pressed a button on whatever it was he was holding, causing the instrument to emit a high-pitched whine and shine a bright green light. As the light swept over the raised skin, the face made by the burn began to move. The eyes snapped wide open, and the mouth puckered into a sour sneer.

'No!' cried Mae. 'It's happening again!' She tried to pull her wrist away from the Doctor's grasp, to hide the face from view – but he held her arm firm.

'I'm going to hurt you, girl!' growled the face of Grandma Betty as it bulged out of the skin on Mae's arm. 'I'm going to hurt you bad! I'm going to make you pay for every moment you spent coveting my savings!'

'But I didn't want any of it,' blubbed Mae. 'I just wanted you to be well again.'

The face twisted and contorted as it grew in size, looking for all the world as though the old woman was trapped beneath the skin of Mae's forearm, trying to force her way out.

Clara looked up and met the Doctor's gaze. 'Doctor?'

'A sentient burn!' proclaimed the Doctor. 'An injury that can talk! A wound with a view!' His eyes lit up at the final analogy. 'It's a new one on me.'

'So what do we do?'

'What we always do,' said the Doctor matter-of-factly. 'We give it a chance.' He twisted Mae's arm round so that the now almost fully formed head was facing him.

'My name is the Doctor,' he said. 'Who or what are you?'

The face turned its scarlet eyes towards the Doctor. 'I am the girl's grandmother, of course.'

'No,' said the Doctor with a shake of his head. 'Whatever you are, you are most definitely *not* Grandma Betty – unless, of course, Grandma Betty was born on a distant world and travelled thousands of light years to come here and start a family…'

He lowered Mae's arm as a sudden thought occurred. 'She wasn't, was she?'

Mae blinked through her tears. 'What? No!'

'And she wasn't made of plastic? Had a hand that flipped open with a gun inside?'

Mae stared at the strange man as if he was insane. 'What are you talking about?'

'I guess not, then!' The Doctor raised the face to his again. 'So I'd like you to tell me the truth. Who are you, and what do you want?'

The face hissed angrily and began to sink back into the skin of Mae's arm.

'Oh, no you don't!' cried the Doctor, blasting Betty with his medical tool and dragging the face back out into the open. 'It's very rude to walk off in the middle of a conversation! Now, tell me who you are.'

When the face spoke again, its voice had changed. It was deeper, more resonant – and it seemed to come from all around the room at the same time. 'The Shroud shall feast!'

'The Shroud…' said the Doctor. 'Never heard of you. How many of you are there? And what's this feast?'

Before the Shroud could reply, the door to the office opened and a middle-aged woman with short, sensible hair entered. She was wearing a white coat and also had a stethoscope draped around her neck.

'What are you doing in my office?' she demanded.

The Doctor flicked off the green light. 'It's OK,' he said confidently. 'I'm the Doctor.'

'No,' retorted the woman. 'I'm the doctor.'

Clara jumped to her feet with a smile. 'And I'm a nurse,' she said, holding out her hand, 'but I'm undercover at the moment, in plain clothes.'

The woman looked down at Mae, who shrugged. 'I don't know who either of them are, or what they're talking about. I just came here to get my burn treated.'

'And now look what's happened to it!' cried the Doctor. Mae looked back at her arm to discover that the Shroud had now disappeared. All that remained was the original face-shaped burn mark.

'I will ask you again,' the woman said firmly, 'and, this time, I expect the truth. What are you people doing in my office?'

The Doctor's eyes grew wide. '*Your* office? Oh! In that case, you must be…' he steered the chair back to the desk and began to rifle through the piles of paperwork. 'Dr Mairi Ellison. Ooh, that's a good name! Mairi!' He rolled it around his mouth few times, trying different inflections. 'MAIri! MaiRI! MAIRI! A name so Scottish, you can almost chew on it!' He leapt up and kissed the air on either side of the confused doctor's face. 'I'm absolutely delighted to meet you, Mairi! You've got a lovely office here, but your desk could do with a tidy up.'

'Oh, well… OK,' said Dr Ellison. 'Did I hear you say that you were a doctor as well?'

'You most certainly did,' beamed the Doctor, wiggling the end of his stethoscope in the air. 'I'm a doctor as well.'

'That still doesn't explain what you're doing in my office.'

'Ah! Well…' The Doctor looked to Clara for an explanation, but she just shrugged. 'I, er… That's it! Yes! I wanted a second opinion.'

'On what?'

The Doctor grabbed Mae's wrist again and held the burn out towards Dr Ellison. 'What do you make of this?'

Dr Ellison pulled a pair of spectacles from her coat pocket and slipped them on. 'It's a scald,' she said, examining the mark. 'Pretty nasty one, too.' She looked up at Mae. 'What was it? Coffee?'

Mae nodded.

Dr Ellison removed her glasses. 'Yes, I thought so. I did much the same thing to my own arm last year.'

'Did you?' asked the Doctor, twirling his strange medical tool in his free hand. 'But the question is, could yours do this?'

He let loose another burst of green light and

began to drag the face of Grandma Betty out from Mae's arm once more. It began to roar angrily.

Dr Ellison backed away in terror. 'What is that?'

'This?' asked the Doctor, holding up his bizarre implement. 'It's called a sonic screwdriver. It uses sound waves to vibrate a rare crystal found only in—'

'Not that,' interrupted Dr Ellison, pointing at Grandma Betty. 'That!'

'Oh, they're called the Shroud,' said the Doctor, 'but aside from that I've no idea. I do know, however, that it must be hidden from sight at once. Do you think you could dress Mae's wound for me? I'll do my best to keep Betty under control while you work.'

Flicking from one setting on his sonic screwdriver to another, the Doctor fired burst after burst at the bulging face until one of them had the desired effect of forcing the Shroud to retreat back into Mae's forearm.

'Now!' cried the Doctor, holding the sonic steady.

Dr Ellison grabbed a first-aid kit from her desk and, with trembling fingers, she laid a sheet of gauze over the burn mark, then began to wrap a bandage around Mae's arm to keep it in place.

'Will that work?' Clara asked the Doctor. 'If the face is hidden from view, will it leave Mae alone?'

'Haven't got a clue,' the Doctor replied. 'But at the moment, it's the best I can think of. The Shroud must be the reason the TARDIS brought us here in the first place, but—'

His words were drowned out by a piercing scream from the corridor outside. He flashed a grin at Clara. 'They're playing our song, dear.'

Clara held out her hand. 'Care to do the corridor quickstep?'

The pair dashed out of the office, closely followed by Dr Ellison and Mae, the wound on her arm now properly dressed.

'This way!' cried the Doctor, racing off in the direction of the scream. But he had only taken a few steps when a second scream rang out – coming from the opposite direction.

The Doctor stopped, turned towards the second scream, and then spun back to face the first. Both were growing in volume and each sounded as urgent as the other. He hopped from foot to foot, jiggling the sonic screwdriver anxiously. 'Argh!'

'It's at times like this we could do with two Doctors!' exclaimed Clara.

'But we do have two doctors,' said Mae.

The Doctor twisted on the spot and grabbed Mae by the shoulders. 'Yes!' he exclaimed. 'Of course! Brilliant! We can split into teams! Mae and I will be Team A... Dr Ellison – Mairi – you and Clara can be Team C.'

'What happened to Team B?' asked Clara.

'Never have a Team B,' said the Doctor earnestly.

'It's like Plan B – always second best. Whereas Plan C and, by extension, Team C, is usually the result of fresh thinking.'

'Team C could stand for Team Clara,' Clara suggested.

The Doctor winked. 'Then Team C rocks!'

And with that, he grabbed Mae's hand and ran off in the direction of the first scream.

The Doctor and Mae found the original screamer in one of the delivery rooms attached to the maternity ward. It was a young, pregnant woman with blonde hair – which was currently plastered to her scalp by a sheen of sweat. She lay with her knees raised on a bed of crumpled, damp sheets – a thin, hospital-issue blanket covering her body.

She stopped screaming as the Doctor entered the room and began to pant heavily. 'Hello, Ruby!' he said, reading the woman's name from the chart hanging above her bed. 'I'm the Doctor. What seems to be the trouble?'

The woman screamed again and grabbed hold of the Doctor's hand, squeezing it in a vice-like grip.

'Ow ow ow ow ow!' The Doctor yelped, trying unsuccessfully to pull his hand away. 'Blimey! Forget nuclear weapons. Send an army of pregnant women over to Cuba and the whole thing will be solved within a day.'

'He's coming!' screeched Ruby between gasping

breaths. 'I can feel it! He's coming!' She screamed again, squeezing the Doctor's hand even harder.

The Doctor whipped out his sonic and used it to relax the woman's fingers long enough to free himself. 'Who's coming, Ruby?' he asked, trying to shake the feeling back into his bruised hand. 'Who?'

'It's possible she might mean this, Doctor,' said Mae, whipping back the blanket to reveal the woman's floral nightdress. There was a large bulge beneath the patterned material.

'Crikey!' said the Doctor, suddenly very uncomfortable. 'That is a new one – in every sense of the word.'

He spotted a nurse lying on the floor at the foot of the woman's bed. 'Oh good!' he cried. 'Something different to look at.' He quickly stooped to examine the nurse with his sonic screwdriver.

Mae took the Doctor's place at the bedside, wetting a towel in a water jug and using it to mop the woman's brow. 'What's wrong with the nurse?' she asked.

'She's fainted,' the Doctor replied. 'Which is a bit odd, when you think about it. You'd imagine she'd be used to this sort of thing.'

'Doctor…' said Mae, slowly backing away from the bed.

The Doctor ignored Mae and tapped the comatose nurse on the cheek. 'Hello?' he called softly. 'Anyone at home?'

'Doctor!'

The Doctor rooted through his pockets and tutted. 'Left my Soborian smelling salts in my wet jacket.'

'*Doctor!*'

'What is it?'

'It's the Shroud!'

The Doctor stood like a startled meerkat, eyes scanning the room. His gaze fell on the pattern of flowers of Ruby's sweat-soaked nightdress. The pictures of daisies on the front of the dress, the part that hung over the soon-to-be-mother's stomach, formed a face. The face of a man. Just like the face in Mae's burn, it began to bulge outwards, the mouth twisting horribly as it snapped open and closed.

'Woman!' the face yelled. 'You know damn well that ain't my baby! I ain't payin' no child support for someone else's kid!'

Ruby turned her face to one side so she could bury it in the pillow and began to cry, her whole body shaking with each sob.

The Shroud's head was now fully formed. It twisted round to glare up at Ruby. 'That's it, woman – keep on cryin'!' it spat. 'That's all you ever do!'

'Oh, my God!' said Mae, almost unable to look. 'Who is that?'

'That's my man, Tyler,' sobbed Ruby. 'But don't listen to a word he says. He *is* the father of my child.'

'I don't doubt it for a second,' said the Doctor. 'I just don't think he's supposed to be in there with it!'

'He was in prison,' said Ruby, 'but they told me he died in a fight.'

'I'm afraid that's likely to be true,' said the Doctor. He stepped up to the bed, sonic held out before him. 'I know you're not really Tyler. You are the Shroud!'

The flower-patterned head turned to glare at the Doctor. 'The Shroud shall feast!' The voice took on the same deeper tone as before and seemed to reverberate from every corner of the room all at once.

'Not in my hospital!' said the Doctor, letting loose with the sonic. The face bellowed like an angry bull and began to sink back into the material of the nightdress. As soon as it had disappeared, the Doctor grabbed the blanket and threw it back over Ruby. 'Do not let anyone get another peek at your nightie,' he said. 'And that's an order.'

He spun his screwdriver like a six-shooter and flashed Mae a wide grin. 'Another one bites the dust!'

Then Ruby screamed again. 'He's coming!' she cried. 'He's coming!'

The Doctor turned with a sigh. 'I told you to keep the blanket on!'

'Er, the blanket is on, Doctor,' said Mae with a smile. 'She's talking about someone else this time.'

The Doctor looked confused for a second, then his eyes widened. 'Ah!'

He dashed to the door of the delivery room and looked both ways along the corridor. 'Hello? Bit of an emergency here!' There was no reply. 'Baby on the way?' Nothing. 'Free biscuits!'

'Free biscuits?' said Mae.

The Doctor shrugged. 'That one would have worked for me.' He dropped to his knees beside the unconscious nurse and tapped her cheeks again, harder this time. There was no reaction. 'Oh, you're no good to me.'

Resigned to his fate, the Doctor removed his jacket and straightened his bow tie. 'Mae,' he directed. 'Get me some clean towels, lots of hot water and something to bite on.'

'Doctor, you're delivering a baby not amputating a leg – and this isn't Victorian England!' said Mae. 'Ruby won't need anything to bite on.'

'I know,' said the Doctor, swallowing hard. 'That's for me.'

20 August 1929

Benjy ran as fast as his young legs would carry him, revelling in the warm, late-summer breeze on his face and the joyful barks of Tess at his side. His sneakers swished through the grass, and his shadow stretched out long and thin ahead of him in the early evening sun. Soon, he and Tess would have to turn and head for home – but he wanted to reach the fence first. The sturdy wooden barrier marked the boundaries of the ranch, and in many ways, Benjy's childhood itself.

The fence was as far as his father allowed him to go when he had finished his chores around the house. For some reason, Ben was always nervous about what might be waiting for him on the other side. Of course, that was old Mrs Grady's land

and she didn't take kindly to trespassers – but he knew that wasn't it. It was as though he was safe on one side of the fence, but not on the other. Still, he wasn't going to waste time worrying about that on a beautiful day like today.

He knew that fall was just over the horizon, with all the work it required on the land, along with a return to the schoolroom and lessons long forgotten over yet another seemingly endless summer. He longed to see his friends again, of course. To splash about in the lake with them before the weather turned too cold, and then to waste away entire weekends lazing at the edge of the fishing hole. But until then, the only things that mattered in this world were a boy and his dog.

There was the fence. Despite the stitch burning into his side, Benjy put on a final burst of speed, determined to reach it before Tess did. She was an old dog now, retired from her working days with his father, and kept as the family pet. He looked down at her now as he ran, her dark eyes wide with the sheer thrill of the adventure. The two of them running together once again.

Benjy reached the fence first, slapping his hand against the rough wood as a way of securing his win. He fell back against it, his breath ragged and his cheeks red from the exercise. Tess barked happily and leapt up at him, her front paws reaching his chest, and he threw his arms around her, holding her tight, but still mindful not to put pressure on the hard lump swelling out of her stomach. She yelped if you even accidentally touched it nowadays, and the last thing he wanted to do was hurt her.

They tumbled down into the cool grass together and Tess shot forward to lick Benjy's face with her long, rough tongue. He laughed and made to push her away, but he didn't keep the distance for long and, within a minute or two, he found himself wiping warm slobber from his face once more.

His breath finally calming, Benjy flipped himself over onto his back and stared up at the few clouds that dotted the otherwise clear, blue sky. He plucked a long blade of grass from the soil and popped it into the corner of his mouth, just the way his father did. Tess lay on her side – she couldn't lie comfortably on her stomach any more – her head nestled in the crook of his elbow, panting hard.

'You know, someday I'm gonna leave this place, old girl,' said Benjy, the grass twitching with each word. 'I know Daddy wants me to stay here and become a ranch hand. He won't quit talkin' about it.' He lowered his voice in an attempt at an impersonation. 'Son, you gotta learn the business from the dust up, just the way I did and my daddy did and his daddy did before him!' He paused to switch the blade of grass to the other side of his mouth. 'But that ain't for me.'

Tess yawned widely and settled back down

against his arm, her breathing slow and regular. 'I'm headin' to the big city, Tess – and I'm takin' you with me when I go. I won't spend my life chasin' cattle, no sir. I'm gonna make somethin' out of myself. Maybe I'll be a clerk in a city bank like Miss Hunnerford's brother, or work in a corner drugstore and meet all kinds of interesting folks. Who knows?'

Benjy fell silent, his gaze swimming from one cloud to the next, trying to identify familiar shapes in them. That one over in the direction of the church looked a little like a jack rabbit – if it had been in a fight and only had one ear left. And that big one just coming over the horizon was a dead ringer for the circus tent that had pitched up in town back in the spring. He closed his eyes and pictured himself back there – a stick of cotton candy in one hand, and a ticket to the show in the other. He'd sat next to Jane from school on the crowded, wooden benches and – as the tumblers entertained the audience from the ring below – he'd abandoned his cotton candy to take her hand in his and squeeze it tightly. He could almost feel it there, right now…

'Benjamin! Benjamin, wake up!'

Benjy's eyes snapped open, and he found himself in the dark. Had he slept past nightfall? If he had, he was late for supper and in for another lecture from his mother. But no – the sun was still out, if a little lower in the sky. There was a shadow lying over him. The shadow of a tall man in a wide hat.

Pushing himself up onto his elbows, Benjy squinted up at the figure standing over him. 'Daddy?' Tess, still lying beside him, rolled herself gingerly onto her stomach and climbed to her feet.

'I was hoping I'd find you out here,' said his father, leaning against the fence and resting a dusty, booted foot up on one of the wooden struts. 'Tess, too.'

Benjy clambered to his feet, noticing his father's horse nearby, grazing on the long grass. He must have been deep asleep not to have heard them coming. 'Why's that, Daddy?'

His father waited a long time before answering. 'Mr Williams, the veterinarian, came over to take a look at one of the calves. The scrawny one that never leaves its mother's side, and got the eye infection a while back.'

'I know the one. Is it OK?'

His father nodded. 'The calf is fine. But Mr Williams also had the results from the tests he ran on Tess a few weeks back.' Responding to her name, the dog padded over so the rancher could reach down and scratch her behind one of her ears.

'Did he bring medicine for her?'

'Nope.'

'Then what?' Benjy looked down at Tess, suddenly nervous. 'Is he going to take her back to his office and operate on her? You said he might have to do that.'

His father turned, and it was then that Benjy realised he was carrying his shotgun. 'Tess is an old dog, Benjy,' he said. 'She's had her time, and now she's sick.'

Tears began to sting Benjy's eyes. 'But she can get well!' he exclaimed. 'I know she can.'

'No, she can't,' said her father firmly. 'And it ain't fair to let her suffer.' Standing up straight, he opened the breach on the shotgun and pulled a shell from his coat pocket.

Benjy grabbed his father's arm, panicking. 'No, Daddy!' he pleaded. 'You can't!'

His father shook his arm free. 'I will do what has to be done!' he said, slotting the shell into place and snapping the shotgun closed. 'Tess is a working dog, and she deserves to be treated with respect – and if that means ending her pain, then that is what I will do.'

The tears were flowing freely down Benjy's face now. He called Tess to him and held her again, his voice little more than a hoarse whisper. 'Please, Daddy! No!'

'Now, you can either be a man about it and help me find a pleasant shady spot for Tess's final resting place, or you cry like a baby and run home to your momma. Which is it to be?'

Tess began to lick the tears from Benjy's cheeks.

'Well, boy?'

Chapter 5

Clara and Dr Ellison found the source of their scream in an empty side ward at the far end of the corridor. To their surprise, it wasn't a patient.

'Who is it?' hissed Clara as they approached a young male doctor backed against the open window, staring down in horror at something beside one of the beds. Tears were streaming down his face. 'Do you know him?'

'Andrew Ross,' replied Dr Ellison. 'He's a junior here, just out of training. I've been working as his mentor for the past few months.' She called out to him. 'Andrew. It's Mairi. What's wrong?'

But the young doctor didn't answer. His eyes remained locked to something on the floor.

'OK,' said Clara calmly. 'Andrew... we're coming

to you…' She began to edge her way around the end of the bed, Dr Ellison behind her – then they saw what he was staring at.

A burst blood bag lay on the ground, its contents spilled into a sticky red puddle. And from that puddle, a head rose up. It was the head of a young woman, possibly beautiful – but it was difficult to tell. The bloody head gazed up at Andrew Ross with a lascivious smile and licked its scarlet lips.

'I never loved you, Andy,' it said. 'I wanted you to find out about me and Chet all along!'

'No! Please, Sophie,' Andrew begged. 'Please… no.'

Dr Ellison paled. 'Oh my God!'

'What is it?' asked Clara. '*Who* is it?'

'His wife, Sophie,' Dr Ellison explained. 'Or at least, she was. She was killed in a car accident – with another man. She told Andrew she was going to Austin to look after her sick mother, but ended up beneath the wheels of a truck on her way to a Fort Worth motel. It destroyed him. He's only just returned to work.'

'Get something to cover it up,' said Clara. Dr Ellison ran to the nearest bed and began to pull off the sheet.

'I forgive you, Sophie,' cried Andrew, pressing himself further back against the window frame. 'I don't care who you were seeing behind my back. I know you didn't mean to hurt me.'

'Forgive me?' slavered the head. 'I don't want your forgiveness. I want him!'

'Andrew!' said Clara. 'Don't listen to it. That's not Sophie. It's called the Shroud, and I think it's trying to upset you. Don't let it do that.'

But Andrew continued to stare in horror at the head of his dead wife.

'All those nights I waited at home alone,' snarled the glistening head. 'You drove me to it, Andy! You drove me into another man's arms!'

'But I had to work late,' Andrew said, the words almost soundless. 'I had patients to treat.'

'And I had a husband – but he wasn't man enough for the job!'

Andrew's face crumpled. 'Please, come back to me, Sophie!' he cried, sitting back on the frame of the open window, the breeze ruffling the back of his shirt.

Dr Ellison dodged around Clara and tossed the sheet over the pool of blood. The head beneath it began to sink back into the ground.

'Andrew!' Dr Ellison called, holding out a hand. 'Come away from the window. It's gone now.'

'I...I dropped a blood bag,' said Andrew, blinking away his tears. 'It burst open and covered the floor – and there was a face. Sophie's face!'

'It's OK,' Dr Ellison soothed.

'No, it is not OK!' spat a voice. The three of them turned back to look at the sheet on the floor – the blood was starting to soak into it. The face was reforming. 'If you hadn't forced me into sneaking around like a guilty schoolgirl, I'd still be alive!'

'*No!*' pleaded Andrew, turning to look at the ground, several stories below. 'It's not true!'

Dr Ellison stepped forward, her own eyes growing wet. 'Andrew,' she said. 'Whatever you think is happening, it's not real. Take my hand and we can talk.'

Andrew Ross raised his eyes once more, gazing into those of his mentor. 'I'm sorry,' he said quietly. 'I have to be with her.' Then he tumbled backwards out into the air.

The Doctor cradled the new-born baby in his arms and grinned. 'And after all that, it's a girl!'

Mae fussed around Ruby, mopping her brow and straightening the bed sheets. 'What are you going to name her?' she asked. 'Have you thought of anything yet?'

Ruby shrugged. 'I always figured it was going to be a boy, named after his daddy.'

'What?' said the Doctor. 'Scary-flowery-nightdress-head? I think the other children might tease her at school.'

The baby gave a gurgle.

'Oh, all right,' said the Doctor. 'There's no need to use language like that.' He handed the baby over to her mother. 'She says her name is *Kill-a-Tron 3000*, but I think a more suitable day-to-day version would be Betty.' He offered Mae a wink, then noticed the nurse at the end of the bed was beginning to come round.

'Oh, *now* you decide to wake up!' he cried. He helped the nurse into a chair. 'You'll be just fine in twenty minutes,' he said kindly. Then he noticed Clara standing in the doorway.

'Hello!' he beamed, standing up. 'We've had a great time here. How about you?'

Clara shook her head.

'Ah. Dr Ellison?'

'She's… She's gone to be with someone. A friend. A… A late friend.'

As Clara spoke, more screams and cries for help began to ring out.

'We have to find out what's going on here and put a stop to it,' said the Doctor. 'Why this hospital? Why now?'

'It's not just the hospital,' said Mae. 'Remember my Grandma Betty? That's how I got this burn in the first place, and it didn't happen here.'

The Doctor grabbed his jacket. 'Show me!'

There were more screams and bulging faces as they ran back along the hospital corridors towards the TARDIS. A child's head stretched out from the lumps in a bowl of oatmeal; the face of an elderly man twisted as it rose from a trolley of soiled sheets; and the sullen woman Clara had seen earlier knelt, sobbing, beside the head of a young soldier as it rose from her scattered bouquet of flowers.

The Doctor tried to help them all as he ran, letting off blast after blast from his sonic at each and every face – but there were just too many of them. He had to find the source of the problem and stop it there.

The trio turned the corner to reach the TARDIS and froze. There, pushing its way out from the pattern of mud spattered on the doors, was another human head. The Doctor grabbed Mae and Clara and dragged them back out of view. 'Oh, brilliant,' he hissed. 'Just what we need.'

Clara nodded, her eyes closed and the back of her neck pressed against the cold stone of the wall. 'Uncle Reuben.'

The Doctor turned to her. 'Uncle who?'

'Uncle Reuben,' said Clara. 'Not a real uncle – a friend of the family kind of uncle. I really loved him, though.'

'No, no, that's not right,' said the Doctor. 'That wasn't your Uncle Reuben. That was Astrid.'

'You said that name before. Who's Astrid?'

The Doctor sighed. 'Astrid Peth. A waitress who pushed a megalomaniac into a warp engine with a forklift truck so I could stop the *Titanic* from crashing into Buckingham Palace on Christmas Day.' He looked away from Clara's stunned expression. 'Actually, saying it in one breath like that makes it almost sound unlikely.'

'Yeah,' said Clara, raising an eyebrow. 'Almost.'

'You're both wrong,' Mae insisted. 'It was Grandma Betty again.'

The Doctor's eyes lit up. 'Now that is fascinating!' he said. 'We each saw someone different in the mud on the doors.' He turned to Clara again. 'Which, by the way, is typical of you. An entire planet filled with bubble bath, and you still manage to get the TARDIS dirty!'

'Stop fussing!' Clara cried. 'Once we're done here, we'll fly it to the Planet of the Car Washes, or something.'

'Fly it?' said Mae, rubbing her forehead. 'Planets filled with bubble bath and car washes? What are you two talking about? Is it some kind of secret code?'

'I'll explain when we're not surrounded by hideous heads,' promised Clara. 'In the meantime, what are we going to do about the face on the TARDIS door?'

The Doctor grinned. 'We look again – just for a second!'

So Clara, Mae and the Doctor popped their heads back around the corner – one above the other – to get another look at the muddy face. Then they disappeared again.

'OK,' said the Doctor. 'Who did you see?'

'Grandma Betty,' said Mae.

'Uncle Reuben,' said Clara. 'You?'

'Astrid Peth,' said the Doctor.

'But how?' asked Clara. 'How are we all seeing different people?'

'The Shroud must be using psychic connections,' said the Doctor. 'Stretching out with mental tentacles – ooh, that is good! Mental tentacles! Remind me to say that again. Stretching out until they touch upon another mind, then they use that person's memories to form a familiar face. My guess is each Shroud starts out as a random face within a pattern, but they're constantly reaching out and probing until they find a victim. Then once a connection is made, they scour your mind for someone that you know – someone that you miss – and use your memories of that person to ensnare you.'

'That's horrible!' exclaimed Clara.

The Doctor nodded his agreement. 'It's similar to how my psychic paper works, only in a nasty, fishing-for-unhappy-memories way.'

'So one of those things grabbed me with its tentacle things?' asked Mae. 'That's why I saw my grandma?'

'Yes, but you fought it,' said the Doctor. 'And you're still fighting it.'

'But what are these Shroud things?'

'They're aliens,' said the Doctor matter-of-factly.

Mae slumped back against the wall. 'Now I know I've gone mad,' she said. 'I could just about cope with my dead grandmother bursting out of my arm

– but now you're talking about little green men from Mars?'

'I'm pretty sure they're not from Mars,' said the Doctor. 'And they're not green, as far as I can tell. Although, the aliens that *are* from Mars *are* actually green, which is interesting. But they're not little. And they hissssssss a lot when they speak.'

Clara spotted Mae's expression of bemusement and stepped in. 'I know it's hard to believe,' she said, 'but aliens are real. I've met a few now and, by and large, they're very nice people.'

The Doctor adjusted his bow tie with a smirk.

'You must have heard of the story – back in the 1940s,' Clara continued. 'The crashed spaceship in Roswell. Area 51, I think they call it.'

'Roswell, New Mexico?' scoffed Mae. 'But that was just a hoax.'

The Doctor snorted back a laugh. 'It most definitely was not a hoax. I told them they needed better shields protecting their thermo couplings, but did they believe me? No! And look where it got them.'

'You have to trust the Doctor on this one,' Clara said kindly. 'He's right.'

Mae took a deep breath and sighed. 'OK,' she said. 'Until I hear a better explanation for what's going on around here – they're aliens, but *not* from Mars!'

The Doctor beamed. 'That's the spirit.'

'So what now?'

'We have to get inside the TARDIS.'

'TARDIS?' asked Mae.

'His blue box,' said Clara. She turned to the Doctor. 'How do we get past the freaky face and its mental tentacles?'

'Oi!' scolded the Doctor. 'Get your own cool phrase!' He thought for a second. 'The face is made of mud, so we take a tip from Clara and...' He darted across the corridor and bathed the lock of a door marked 'Janitor' in pulsing green light from the sonic. There was a faint *click*, and the door swung open to reveal a mop, bucket and industrial-sized cans of liquid soap. 'Voila!'

'You're never going to let me forget that, are you?' said Clara.

The Doctor shook his head. 'I certainly hope not.'

The trio armed themselves with cleaning supplies and filled the bucket with water from a cracked sink fixed to the rear wall of the closet. 'OK,' whispered the Doctor. 'On three... *Three!*'

They leapt around the corner together, the head bulging out of the mud stain again, screaming in rage at the sight of them. 'Watch out for the mental tentacles,' warned the Doctor, trying to control the face with his screwdriver. 'Don't let them attach themselves to you.'

'Now!' cried Clara – and Mae hoisted up the bucket of now soapy water, tossing it all over the front of the TARDIS and smothering the writhing, angry head in suds. Clara brought the mop down hard, pushing against the now pliable skull of the Shroud and pushing back into the door.

'Almost there!' yelled the Doctor, stepping closer to the shrinking face and turning the sonic up a notch. Clara began to mop furiously at the stain as muddy water lapped around their feet until – eventually – the stain and the face were gone.

'Yes!' exclaimed Clara and Mae together, dropping the mop and bucket in order to hug. The Doctor raised his hand for a high five, realised he wasn't going to get one, and pretended to stretch.

'OK,' he said, slipping his screwdriver away. 'Let's get to Mae's office and the bottom of all this...' He unlocked the TARDIS and darted inside, racing for the console.

Clara stepped back to allow Mae to go inside next. The reporter stood, mouth agape as the impossibility of it all swept over her. 'It's... It's bigger on the inside!' she gawped.

'Careful,' said Clara quietly, joining her and closing the door. 'Don't let him hear you talk about her that way. You'll never hear the end of it.'

Mae watched as Clara hurried to join the Doctor in the centre of the room at some sort of – well, she had no words to describe what it was. Some kind of six-sided desk covered in buttons, switches and levers. She approached cautiously.

'Hang on,' said Clara. 'I thought the helmet thing was kaput?'

'Helmic regulator,' corrected the Doctor, his fingers twitching like an eager secretary waiting to take dictation, 'and it is, but we don't need it for this journey.'

'What is this place?' asked Mae, taking a step forward, but not quite daring to approach the console.

'The TARDIS!' beamed the Doctor, puffing out his chest. 'Time And Relative Dimension In Space. Isn't she lovely?'

'It's a spaceship,' Clara elaborated, giving him a look. 'And a time machine – all rolled into one. Although, it's not a time machine at the moment. He thinks I made the TARDIS cry, so that bit's not working now.'

'But she can still do all the space stuff!' the Doctor pointed out.

Mae looked nervously from the Doctor to Clara and back again. 'You don't work at the hospital, do you?' she asked, edging away. 'You're *in* the hospital. The psychiatric ward! That's why I can't understand a word either of you says!'

She stopped as an idea cascaded over her. 'Oh, my God! I'm in the psych ward with you, aren't I? All those faces – they're all in my head. I've gone mad!'

The Doctor hurried over to Mae and took her

hand. Then he pinched the skin on the back of it.

'Ow!'

'See,' the Doctor smiled. 'You're not imagining anything. I know it's a lot to take in, but this is all actually happening.'

'Really?'

'Really. And what Clara said was true. The TARDIS can't travel through time until I repair her, but she can move across space. To the furthest reaches of the universe. Now, where did you first see Grandma Betty's face this morning?'

'On my desk, at my office.'

'Which is…?'

'The *Morning News*. Young Street. About four miles away.'

The Doctor blinked. 'Four miles?'

Mae nodded.

'Yes, well – that's not even trying, is it?' muttered the Doctor, dropping Mae's hand and heading back to the console. 'Still – it'll give the old girl a bit of fresh air…' He tapped the address into the keyboard. '*Dallas Morning News*… Young Street… Dallas, Texas…' He switched to another of the six sides to attack a series of switches and toggles, spinning like a bow-legged ballerina as he did so. 'Fuelling the thermo buffer, flash updating the nano-ram, and let's give it a bit of choke as it's cold out there today!'

He winked to Mae, then threw back the flight lever…

VWOR-VWO-VWO-VWO-WO-WO-WO-WO-W-
W-W-W-W!

The TARDIS engines rose and fell like a car with a dying battery.

'What?' The Doctor flipped a few more switches, then tried the lever again.

VWOR-VWOR-VWOR-VWO-VWO-VWO-VWO-
WO-WO-WO-WO-W-W-W-W!

'No, no, *no!*'

'You can't blame this one on me!' snapped Clara.

The Doctor turned to reply, but resorted instead to wagging his forefinger like a stern teacher. He went back to fiddling with the controls.

'What's wrong with it?' asked Mae.

'There's nothing wrong,' said the Doctor, exasperated. 'She just won't take off.'

Mae smiled. 'So it can't travel in space, either?'

'Yes, she can,' cried the Doctor, 'but something is stopping us from dematerialising.' He raced round to the monitor and switched it on, crossing his fingers that he wouldn't be confronted by another face from the past. The screen hissed for a second, then burst into life. 'There!' he said, jabbing a long finger at the screen. 'That's what's affecting us.'

Both Clara and Mae hurried to join him.

'Is that the Earth?' Mae asked, looking up at the monitor.

'A live picture,' confirmed the Doctor. 'I've hacked into a camera on one of the Sputnik satellites.'

'But that planet has rings around it,' said Mae. 'That looks like Saturn, not the Earth.'

'Those aren't rings,' explained the Doctor. 'It's a wormhole, or one end of it, at least.' He flicked the monitor off and rested his forehead against the screen. 'That's why the TARDIS won't take off. It's just too dangerous.'

'But in all the sci-fi books I've ever read, a wormhole is like a tunnel through space,' said Clara.

The Doctor nodded. 'Yes, yes, very good.'

'And the end of that one is surrounding the whole planet?'

The Doctor began to make shapes with his fingers in the air. 'Imagine a giant doughnut,' he said, waving his hand in an exaggerated circle, then suddenly scrubbing it out. 'Actually, don't. It's nothing like that. Forget the doughnut. It's more like a scotch egg. Anyway – the point is that there is a wormhole connected to the Earth, leading from… somewhere.'

'Is that how the Shroud are getting here?' asked Mae.

'I'd bet my bow tie on it,' said the Doctor. 'And you saw them first at your desk this morning. I need to get a look at that desk.'

'But the TARDIS won't take off,' said Clara.

The Doctor arched an eyebrow 'Then we need to find another mode of transport…'

Chapter 6

It turned out to be quite easy to steal the ambulance. The driver was already distracted, staring sadly into a face which had pushed its way out of the gravel edging to the parking lot. So all the Doctor had to do was sonic the engine into life and they were away. Mae gave him directions to the newspaper office.

The scene out on the streets was every bit as bad as inside the hospital. Faces of the Shroud were bulging out all around them, trapping their victims with their psychic probes. People stared in horror at them, tears streaming down their faces.

'This is terrible!' cried Clara, standing in the back of the ambulance and clinging on to the seats. 'We have to help them.'

'We will,' the Doctor assured her. 'We can't deal

with each face individually – for every one we get rid of, dozens more would sprout up. I have to get to the source and stop it from there.'

'Like turning off a faucet?' said Mae.

'Exactly,' beamed the Doctor. 'A freaky face-filled faucet!'

'I don't get it,' said Mae. 'I've seen faces in things ever since I was little. There was one on the pattern of my wallpaper when I was a kid, and another made of mildew on the bathroom ceiling of my dorm room at college. It always came back, no matter how many times I washed it away. None of my roommates ever seemed to notice it, though. Or attempted to clean it up, for that matter.'

'Some people are more susceptible to psychic influences,' explained the Doctor. He spun the steering wheel to avoid an elderly woman kneeling in the road, deep in conversation with the head of a young boy peeking out from behind a mailbox. '*You* see a face hidden in a seemingly random design or an arrangement of objects, and other people don't. It just means you're a more powerful receiver than they are.'

'So I've been surrounded by aliens all my life?'

The Doctor nodded. 'You'd be surprised how often that happens.'

'But why?' asked Clara. 'If the Shroud have been here for so long, why wait until now to reveal themselves?'

'I don't know,' admitted the Doctor, 'but I'm going to find out.' Suddenly, he hit the brakes.

'What's wrong?' asked Clara.

'I almost missed it,' said the Doctor, swinging the ambulance around.

'Missed what?'

'That old lady wasn't crying.'

The Doctor pulled up across the street from the woman, and jumped out of the ambulance. 'Hello!' he called, striding over. 'I'm the Doctor. What seems to be the trouble?'

The woman looked up, concern etched across her features. 'This is Sammy,' she said, indicating the young boy hiding in the bushes. 'He lives in my building, two floors above me. I came out to mail a letter and found him here.'

'Hello, Sammy,' said the Doctor. 'Weird day, huh?'

The young boy didn't reply.

'Lots of funny faces poking out from the walls and stuff,' continued the Doctor. 'Did you see any of those?'

Sammy nodded. 'My mom did.'

'Where's your mom now?' asked the Doctor.

'In our apartment,' Sammy replied. 'Talking to my dad.'

'Then why are you out here? Don't you want to talk to your dad, too?'

'My dad's in Heaven. My mom is crying.'

'Ah, I see.'

The elderly woman smiled. 'I asked Sammy if he'd like to come and wait in my apartment until his mom feels better,' she said. 'I thought we could eat cookies and watch cartoons on television together. I've just baked a fresh batch of raisin bran.'

'Now, that sounds like a good idea,' said the Doctor. 'I can't think of anything better to prescribe on a day like this than a good dose of Loony Tunes and raisin bran cookies – and I'm a doctor. What do you say, Sammy?'

The young boy shook his head. 'My mom says I'm not allowed to talk to people I don't know.'

'She sounds very wise,' said the Doctor, 'but I think she wouldn't mind on this occasion. And you do live in the same building as...' he turned to the woman.

'Edith,' she said. 'Edith Thomas.'

The Doctor shook her hand. 'Delighted to meet you, Edith Thomas,' he said. 'Have you seen Edith before today, Sammy?'

The boy nodded. 'I see her when I'm on my way to get the school bus.'

'And what does Edith do when she sees you on your way to school?'

'She smiles at me.'

The Doctor leaned in and whispered. 'Then I think she might be quite friendly. And,' he paused to sniff at the woman, 'from the smell of her, those cookies are going to be great! Now, how about if you go with Edith back to her apartment and watch some cartoons? Then I'll find a way to cheer your mom up, and you can go back upstairs.'

Sammy eyed the Doctor cautiously. 'You can help my mom feel better?'

'I'm the Doctor. I make everyone feel better.'

'OK...' said the boy, accepting Edith's hand. The Doctor watched as she led him inside the apartment building, then returned to the ambulance.

They drove in silence for a few blocks. Mae stared out of the window, running her fingers over the bandage covering her wound. 'I wasn't after her money,' she said eventually. 'What my grandma said about me earlier. It wasn't true.'

'That face wasn't your grandma,' said the Doctor. 'It was just using your memories of her to upset you.'

Mae felt her eyes begin to grow wet again. 'Well, it worked.'

'Don't let it,' said the Doctor. 'That's what the Shroud wants. To feed on your sorrow.'

'It feeds on *grief*?' said Mae, looking bewildered.

'As far as I can tell,' said the Doctor. 'And it's ravenously hungry.'

'Is that why we all saw someone different on the TARDIS door?' asked Clara.

'It was reaching out to all three of us,' said the Doctor. 'Trying to decide which of us was easiest to manipulate. Which of us would provide it with the tastiest meal.'

Clara looked shocked. 'But messing with your memories like that. It's…'

'It's horrible,' finished the Doctor, 'and incredibly difficult. It means the Shroud are powerful. Powerful enough to twist your memories of a loved one, like it did with Mae. It uses guilt to add to the sense of loss you already feel.'

He turned a corner and hit the brakes again. There was a police car blocking the road.

'Sorry,' said Mae, 'I forgot. We can't go through Dealey Plaza, the police still have it sealed off after yesterday.'

Suddenly, the Doctor slapped his palm to his forehead. 'Why didn't I think of it sooner?' he cried. 'Yesterday! The assassination of President Kennedy! The entire country is in mourning. That's what the Shroud have been waiting for.'

'Why?' asked Clara. 'What does that have to do with all this?'

'Everything,' replied the Doctor. 'The faces have been around for years, hanging about, looking all freaky. But they were waiting for something. Something that would give them enough energy to make that final push through from the wormhole.'

'A national tragedy,' said Mae.

'A global tragedy,' said the Doctor. 'The entire world grieving. It's like we've laid on a giant banquet for the Shroud.'

'That's why I know the name of the hospital!' exclaimed Clara. 'We learned all about it at school. Parkland Memorial was where they took the President's body for his autopsy. No wonder everyone looked so down when we first arrived.'

'And Mae's office has been covering the story,' said the Doctor. 'What were you doing just before you first saw the face of your grandmother?'

'Looking through some photographs of the shooting,' said Mae. 'They were horrible.'

'And they upset you?'

'Of course!'

'That's why your office and the hospital were affected first,' said the Doctor, reversing the ambulance back up the street. 'The places where emotion is strongest will be the weakest points for the Shroud to break through.'

'But it's spreading fast,' said Clara, 'and, like you said, it's a global tragedy. That means…'

'The same thing is going to happen all over the world,' said the Doctor. 'We have to get to Mae's office now. If we can't stop this, then no one will ever smile again.'

'It was right there,' said Mae, pointing to the coffee stain at the edge of her desk. 'I saw it!'

The Doctor buzzed the sonic screwdriver over the collection of brown rings and marks, then checked the results. 'Well, there's nothing there now,' he said. 'Nothing but bad coffee and old varnish.' He turned to Clara. 'How about you?' he asked. 'Any sign of your uncle?'

Clara shook her head. 'Nothing.'

'Same here,' said the Doctor. 'No Astrid.'

'But that's good, isn't it?' asked Mae. 'That means it's gone back down that hole thing?'

'Or come out completely,' said the Doctor. He fired the sonic again, this time using it to sweep around the office.

The news floor was deserted when they arrived. Mae had found Jim, the young sports reporter, sobbing on the stairs as the face of his father yelled abuse at him from the carpet. The Doctor had thrown Jim's jacket over the head and held it in place with his screwdriver long enough for Clara to lead the boy outside. They knew the Shroud was likely to capture his mind again before long, but at least they'd given him a brief respite from his sadness.

'Where is everyone?' Clara asked. 'I thought newspaper offices were supposed to be busy.'

'It usually is,' said Mae. 'Even when there's a big story, like yesterday, there's always someone here.'

'Unless they've all been scared away,' said the Doctor, swinging the sonic round again. 'There!' he hissed. 'Can you hear that?'

'No,' said Clara.

Mae shook her head. 'Me neither.'

The Doctor double tapped the handle of the

screwdriver and turned up the volume. The sound immediately became clear.

'Someone's crying,' said Clara.

'Correction,' said the Doctor. 'Someone is crying in here.'

They followed the sound between the desks towards the editor's office. Inside, Ben Parsons was kneeling on the floor, his eyes red with tears. But Ben wasn't alone. Kneeling beside him was a woman. She wore a pale blue dress with a veil across her face that obscured her eyes.

'Ben!' cried Mae, darting forward – but the Doctor grabbed her arm and held her back.

'Don't go near!'

'He's my editor,' said Mae, pulling against the Doctor's grip. 'My friend.'

The Doctor held her firm. 'But she isn't,' he said, gesturing to the woman beside Ben.

'Well, who is she?' asked Clara.

'Any number of people,' said the Doctor. 'Grandma Betty, Uncle Reuben, Astrid Peth. At the moment, I'd imagine she's whoever Ben doesn't want to see.'

Clara gasped. 'That's the Shroud?'

'One of them at least,' said the Doctor.

'That's why it wasn't in the stain on my desk,' said Mae. 'It's out!'

'The next stage of the Shroud's attack,' said the Doctor. 'This must be what they become once they're inside your memories. Stay back.' He released his grip on Mae's arm and crept into the office. Crouching next to the woman, he scanned her with the sonic. 'Basic humanoid biology,' he said, checking the reading. 'With one exception…' He grabbed the end of the veil and raised it.

The woman had sparkling brown eyes; bright, inquisitive – but not at all human.

'They… They look like a dog's eyes!' cried Mae.

'A collie by the look of them,' said the Doctor. 'Could be that Ben saw a dog in the stain where you saw your grandma.'

'But why is she… *it* holding his hand?' asked Clara.

'It's gone deeper,' explained the Doctor. 'Gone inside his mind.' He leaned over and looked at the woman's hand, tightly gripping Ben's. The fingers were long and slender, tipped with nails polished a dark, sparkling blue.

'Then get her out!' cried Mae. 'Pull them apart!' She made to step into the office again, and the Doctor jumped up to stop her.

'I can't,' he said. 'I don't know what damage it would do to Ben if I severed the physical link. It could release him, but it could just as easily kill him.'

'Then what can we do?'

'*We* do nothing,' said the Doctor, slipping his screwdriver away. 'This is down to me.' He stepped up to Ben and realised he was muttering something under his ragged breaths. 'This can't be happening. This isn't happening.'

'Hang on,' said the Doctor. 'I'm coming to help.' He turned to Mae. 'Tell me about him.'

Mae thought hard, suddenly on the spot. 'He's, er… he's called Benjamin Parsons, although he prefers 'Ben'. He's 44, no wait – 45 years old. He's married to Jane, and he's been editor here for almost seven years.'

'Thank you,' said the Doctor, kneeling on the other side of Ben to the blue-veiled woman. 'That could be useful.'

'Wait!' said Clara, firmly. 'You'd better not do what I think you're going to do.'

'That depends,' said the Doctor. 'You might be thinking that I'm about to boil an egg. In which case, you'd be completely wrong.'

'Don't get clever with me,' snapped Clara, ignoring the Doctor's instructions about staying away and striding into the office to glare up at him. 'You're going in there, aren't you? Inside Ben's mind.'

'Just for a quick look around,' said the Doctor. 'It could give me the answer to stopping the Shroud from feeding on him.'

'And if it doesn't? If you get stuck in there?'

'Well, at least I won't be lonely,' smiled the Doctor. 'There'll be three of us – at least!'

'I don't understand,' said Mae as Clara re-joined

her in the doorway. 'He's going *inside* Ben's mind? What does that mean?'

'It means,' said Clara, 'that he's going to do everything he can to save him.'

They watched as the Doctor closed his eyes and took a deep breath. Then he took hold of Ben's free hand and quietly spoke a single word.

'Geronimo.'

20 August 1929

'Now, you can either be a man about it and help me find a pleasant shady spot for Tess's final resting place,' said Benjy's father, 'or you cry like a baby and run home to your momma. Which is it to be?'

Tess began to lick the tears from Benjy's cheeks.

'Well, boy?'

'Could I possibly add a third option?' said a voice. 'Leave this man's memories and never return.'

Mr Parsons spun round. 'Just who in the hell are you?'

'I've been called many names,' said the newcomer as he bent to tickle Tess under the chin. 'Theta Sigma, the Oncoming Storm and, for one rather embarrassing weekend, Mable.' He stood and faced Mr Parsons. 'But most people just call me Doctor.'

'Well, Doctor… Would you care to tell me what you're doing on my land?'

'Now, you see, that's where we hit a bit of a problem,' said the Doctor. 'This isn't your land, you see. This isn't any land at all, in fact.'

'What are you talking about?'

'Oh, it feels like it,' said the Doctor. He jumped up and down a few times, his boots clumping against the dirt. 'I'll give you that. But actually we're inside a memory.' He turned to smile down at Benjy. 'Your memory.'

'My memory?' asked Benjy. 'You mean I'm dreaming?'

'Sort of,' said the Doctor. 'But not the sort of dream you or I usually have. Actually, not the sort of dream I have at all. You want to stay clear of those unless you fancy being chased across Metebelis Three by giant sticks of celery. No, there's an alien in your mind, Ben. An alien called the Shroud that wants to feed on your grief.'

Mr Parsons raised his shotgun and aimed it at the Doctor. 'You'd better shut your mouth if you know what's good for you.'

'I wouldn't fire that in here, if I were you,' the Doctor warned. 'Who knows what damage you could do to Ben's memories? You might get lucky and just wipe out his 7th birthday party, but then maybe you'll hit one of his bad experiences. And you want those intact, don't you?'

'I… I don't understand what's happening!' said Benjy.

The Doctor rested a hand on the boy's shoulder. 'Don't worry. That's just the effect of the Shroud. It's distorting what really happened in your past to try and upset you.'

Mr Parsons released the safety catch on his gun. 'That is enough,' he snarled. 'Whoever you are, you have until the count of ten to turn around and walk away from my son.'

'And there we come to our second problem,' said the Doctor, fixing Mr Parsons with a hard stare. 'One – you're not really his father and, two – I don't do ultimatums.' He pulled his sonic screwdriver from his pocket and aimed a blast at the gun. The weapon dissolved into atoms.

Benjy gasped. 'How did you do that?'

'It wasn't a real gun,' said the Doctor, 'just your memory of the one your father used to have. I simply erased it from your mind by blasting a couple of neurons. Sorry about that. Not strictly something I should do. But then, neither is this…'

The Doctor activated his sonic again. This time, Mr Parsons himself disappeared in an explosion of tiny particles.

Benjy spun to stare up at the Doctor. 'You killed my dad!'

'That wasn't your dad,' said the Doctor. 'It was just an image of him. At first, I thought he must be the Shroud that has invaded your mind – but he couldn't be. He was too surprised to learn that this wasn't really his land. Which means, the parasite must be you!' He pointed his sonic down at Tess the dog.

'Very clever, Doctor!' growled Tess.

Benjy's eyes widened in amazement. 'My dog can talk!'

The Doctor nodded. 'I had a dog that could do that, once. You'd be amazed how quickly the novelty wears off.' He continued to aim his sonic screwdriver at Tess. 'Leave this man's memories, and I will find you and your kind another planet to live on.'

Tess threw her head back and laughed. 'Why should I leave, Doctor? The feast has just begun… Remember, boy…' hissed the dog. 'Remember how you shot me to stop my agony.'

'Not likely,' said the Doctor. 'I've wiped his father's gun from his memory.'

'Then I shall remind him of another gun,' sneered Tess.

Flash!

There was a shimmer in the air and, suddenly, Benjy was holding a plastic ray gun with red lightning bolts painted along the side.

'What?' The Doctor scowled. 'That's a toy space gun! It does nothing scarier than make a silly noise.' He turned and whispered to his sonic screwdriver. 'Not that there's anything wrong with that.'

'Really?' said Tess. The dog turned to her young master. 'Would you care to demonstrate the power of your toy?'

Benjy shrugged, aimed his ray gun at the fence and fired. A purple laser bolt shot from the end with a sound like *Pnew!* The wood exploded into flames.

'That's impossible!' cried the Doctor.

'Not to a child,' said Tess. 'To an 8-year-old boy, a toy gun really works. That's how he remembers it.'

'Then I have to make him forget that as well,' said the Doctor. 'Benjy, this isn't how it happened! The Shroud is manipulating your memories, trying to intensify your grief. You have to remember, Benjy. Remember how it really happened. But you can only do that if you admit to yourself that none of this is real.'

'I don't understand,' said Benjy. 'I'm just a kid.'

'No, you're not,' said the Doctor. 'You're Ben Parsons, the 45-year-old editor of the *Dallas Morning News* newspaper. You're married to Jane, and you love both her and your job very much.'

'Don't listen to him, boy!' snarled Tess. 'You know the truth! You know you're only 8 years old and that you shot your dog to put her out of her misery!'

Ben began to raise the gun again.

'Remember, Ben,' urged the Doctor. 'Remember...'

Benjy paused. 'Wait,' he said, looking down at Tess. 'You said I'm 8 years old, but that ain't right. I was 10, nearly 11. I remember because my dad got me a new puppy for my 11th birthday to replace Tess!'

'That's it!' cried the Doctor with a smile. 'You're doing it.'

'And it didn't happen outdoors near the fence, neither. We were at the ranch, out back by the chicken coop.'

The Doctor grabbed the reins of Mr Parson's horse and leapt up into the saddle. He held a hand down to Benjy. 'Then what say we go there and remember some more, partner!'

Warily, Benjy tossed the ray gun aside. It exploded into sparkling atoms before it hit the dirt. Then he took the Doctor's hand and climbed up into the saddle behind him. 'Let's go!'

The Doctor snapped the reins and they were off, galloping across the plain. Benjy clung on tightly, his arms around the Doctor's waist and his face buried in his back. No, against the shoulder. No, his face was in the Doctor's mass of dark hair!

'Whoa!' exclaimed Ben, looking down at himself. He'd grown over thirty years in as many seconds, and his voice was suddenly deep and booming. 'I guess you were right about me being 45 years old, Doctor!'

'It's a good age, 45,' the Doctor shouted over his shoulder. 'That's how old I was when I left primary school.'

'You cannot defeat me, Doctor!' snarled a voice.

The Doctor and Ben looked down. Tess the dog was racing across the plain alongside the horse.

'I can if I beat you to the ranch,' called the Doctor.

'And how are you going to do that, if Ben can't remember his father's horse?'

The stallion Ben and the Doctor were riding on vanished in a shower of sparkling atoms, and the two men tumbled to the ground. Laughing, Tess the dog ran on towards the farmhouse on the horizon.

'That wasn't fair,' said the Doctor, climbing to his feet and dusting himself down. 'And if the Shroud isn't playing fair, then neither will we.' He turned to Ben. 'There's no reason why we should take the long route. Picture the ranch in your mind. Out back, by the chicken coop...'

Flash!

The Doctor and Ben stepped out of the back door of the ranch house. It was a clear night and the Moon cast an eerie glow over the chicken coop.

There was a man kneeling in the yard, his back to them. 'Mr Williams!' Ben exclaimed. 'The veterinarian.'

The vet stood and turned, the limp body of Tess the dog in his arms. 'Benjy,' he said, surprised. 'Your dad told me you were in bed, asleep.'

Ben turned to the Doctor. 'This is how it really happened,' he said. 'The vet came and—'

Suddenly, Tess raised her head to the sky and howled. '*Noooooo!*'

Flash!

The Doctor and Ben found themselves standing in a dusty old attic, surrounded by boxes and tea chests packed with odds and end.

'Blimey,' said the Doctor. 'It's a bit of a mess in here.'

'Where are we?' asked Ben. 'What is all this stuff?'

'We're in your mind,' said the Doctor. 'These boxes are filled with your memories. The Shroud is trying to make you focus on the bad ones, but you mustn't let it. We have to concentrate on the happy ones.'

'How do we do that?'

'By searching for them,' said the Doctor, beginning to rummage through the nearest box. 'How about this?' he asked, producing a fishing rod.

Flash!

The Doctor and Ben were suddenly sitting in a small boat in the middle of a dark lake. The moonlight glistened on the surface of the oily, black water.

'Oh, no!' said Ben.

'What's wrong?' asked the Doctor.

'This is from when I was 17,' said Ben. 'I came fishing late at night by myself. I'd... I'd had a couple of beers...'

The Doctor glanced down at the collection of empty beer cans in the bottom of the boat. 'A couple?'

'All right,' sighed Ben. 'I came out here to drink

beer. Fishing was just a cover story. I lost my oars, and couldn't get back to shore.'

'And?'

'I was out here all night, at least until the storm came.'

Right on cue, a clap of thunder sounded and raindrops began to ping off the empty cans. But there was another sound, too – a splashing sound. The Doctor looked over the side of the boat to see Tess the dog swimming past.

'I thought I'd have to find a bad memory myself, Doctor,' she said. 'But you've done all the hard work for me.'

'This has gone far enough,' snarled the Doctor. 'I'm sorry, Ben – this may sting a bit…' He whipped out his sonic and aimed a blast at the sky. Then he lashed out with his hand and punched a hole in reality.

Ben winced, as though he'd just taken a bite from a slice of lemon. Through the hole, he could see the dusty attic on the other side. The Doctor slipped the sonic away, grabbed the edges of the tear and ripped it further so it was wide enough for the two men to climb through.

Back in the loft space, the Doctor gestured to the boxes. 'You find something that makes you happy.'

Ben pulled a handful of books from the nearest tea chest, then smiled at something pressed between the pages of one of them. He pulled out a length of string, at the end of which was a deflated red balloon. 'This is a good memory,' he said.

'A burst balloon?' said the Doctor. 'You like to remember about the time a balloon burst? Do you know, I'll never really understand you humans.'

'It's not the balloon itself,' said Ben. 'It's where I got it. On my first proper date with Jane, when I was 21...'

Flash!

The balloon bobbed in the evening air, almost dancing to the sound of the carnival music. The entire town was enjoying the fair.

'Marvellous!' beamed the Doctor, a few steps behind Ben and Jane. He followed them closely as they laughed in the house of mirrors, fired a rifle at the shooting gallery, and screamed through a trip on the ghost train.

'This is brilliant!' yelled the Doctor from the rear seat of their carriage as it whizzed through a dark tunnel, filled with pretend ghosts and ghouls. 'Although I do have to say that real ghosts don't look like that. They're more of a yellowish-white. Something to do with the sulphur build-up in ectoplasm. Oh, and I can see that vampire reflected in the haunted mirror which – frankly – is just a normal mirror with a face painted on.'

After the ghost train – and the five minutes the Doctor spent trying to explain the errors to the operator – they bought ice creams, and wandered over to a striped tent to join an excited crowd gathered outside.

'Roll up, roll up!' cried a side-show operator. 'Come inside and see a miracle of nature – something that should never be!'

Ben and Jane shared a giggle, then hurried inside, the Doctor close behind. They paid their entrance fee, then joined a group of intrigued people inside the darkened interior.

After a few moments, the lights came up and the showman took to a small wooden stage in front of the crowd. 'Ladies and gentlemen!' he exclaimed. 'It is time to reveal a great secret – a secret hidden from mankind for generations…' He gestured to a small cage, covered by a blanket.

The Doctor craned his neck, trying to see around Jane's red balloon.

'Prepare to be astounded and amazed!' The man grabbed the corner of the blanket. 'Man's best friend can finally converse with him!' He pulled the blanket away to reveal a dog inside the cage. It was Tess.

'I'm in so much pain, Ben,' said the dog, pushing the cage door open with her nose and padding over to him. 'Please make it go away.'

Ben looked down at his hands and gasped. He was holding one of the rifles from the shooting gallery. The rest of the audience screamed at the sight of the gun and ran out of the tent, leaving Ben, Jane and the Doctor alone with the talking dog.

'Oh, this is ridiculous!' groaned the Doctor, aiming his sonic at the weapon and dissolving it into atoms. 'I can't follow you through every single one of your memories and make you forget every gun you've ever seen. You're American!'

'You see, Doctor,' growled the Shroud through Tess's canine features. 'You can't win. The Shroud shall feast!'

'There is one other option, though,' said the Doctor. 'I'm sorry, Ben. I know your dog meant a lot to you, but you're going to have to forget her.'

Ben looked down at Tess with sad eyes. 'Really?'

'I'm afraid so. That way, you won't have seen her face in the coffee stain on Mae's desk and the Shroud will have no way to attack you.'

'No!' The fur on Tess's back raised up and she bared her teeth, growling angrily as the Doctor raised his sonic screwdriver.

Then – suddenly – the dog was whisked out of the tent, yelping as though she had been injured.

'Is that it?' asked Ben. 'Is it all over?'

The Doctor examined his sonic. 'It can't be. I didn't do anything.'

'And I can still remember Tess,' said Ben. 'From when I was little, and—'

Without warning, Ben flew out of the tent after his dog, as though being dragged away by some invisible force.

The Doctor spun round as the carnival began

to melt away. First Jane, then the tent, then the attractions outside.

Flash!

'No!' The Doctor sat bolt upright on the carpet and stared down. He had let go of Ben's hand. No, that wasn't possible. Someone had pulled them apart – and done the same with the Shroud on the other side. Ben was lying on the ground between them, twitching. The woman with the blue veil shimmered like sapphires, then vanished.

'Clara!' the Doctor cried, jumping to his feet. 'What happened?' Through the office window, he saw Clara and Mae being led away by two police officers. 'Clara!' She turned back to look at him, only to be pushed out through the newsroom door.

Then someone grabbed the Doctor's hands and handcuffed them behind his back. 'Sir, you are under arrest on suspicion of stealing an ambulance from Parkland Memorial Hospital earlier today…'

'Ben!' shouted the Doctor, pushing the police officer away. He dropped to his knees beside the newspaper editor and rested an ear on his chest. 'His heart has stopped!' the Doctor cried. 'You have to help him. He's dying!'

The police officer drew his gun and pointed it at the Doctor. 'Sir, move away now!'

'Somebody help him!'

Chapter 7

'I did not kill him!' The Doctor leapt up from his chair for the third time in as many minutes. 'And if I'm being honest, I don't think you're listening to a word I've been saying. You have to let me out of here right now. Your planet is under attack and I have to find a way to save it.'

The two police detectives on the other side of the table shared a weary glance. They were both in their late 20s and they both sported the same buzz-cut hairstyle. The only difference between them was the colour of their suits.

'Please take your seat, sir,' said the one in the green suit.

'All right!' said the Doctor, throwing up his hands. 'We'll do it your way.' He sat down and studied the two detectives. 'Which one of you is the bad cop?'

'Excuse me?' said Grey suit.

'The bad cop,' the Doctor repeated. 'The one who's going to threaten to rough me up. Then the other one will send him out for some air and offer to get me a coffee.' He looked hard at the two suits. 'Trust me, it'll speed things up if we just skip that bit.'

Grey suit's eyes narrowed. 'Sir, we are both fully trained in suspect interrogation techniques. Neither one of us is going to threaten you with violence.'

The Doctor slumped back in his seat and sniffed. 'Well, if you're not going to play along, there's not much point us continuing.'

'Let's start at the beginning,' said Green suit. 'As you are no doubt aware, President Kennedy was shot and killed yesterday afternoon. Can you tell us where you were when that incident occurred?'

'I was on an archaeological dig, 400,000 light years away in the 51st century.'

Grey slammed his palm down on the table. 'This is serious!' he shouted.

'I *am* being serious!' the Doctor shouted back, slamming his own palm down on the table. 'And for what it's worth, you're the bad cop – you just don't know it. Now, can we please hurry this up? We're running out of time.'

'Running out of time for what?'

The Doctor stood up and leaned across the table to Grey. 'The faces.'

'What faces?' asked Grey.

'What faces? Hasn't anyone crawled out of your coffee? No one hanging around in the sink when you trimmed your hair this morning?'

'Sir, I think you should sit down,' said Green, giving his colleague a sideways glance. 'Perhaps you aren't feeling very well. Is that it? Would you like us to call a doctor?'

'I *am* a doctor!'

'A doctor of what?' asked Green. 'Medicine?'

'Among other things,' said the Doctor. 'Many other things, actually. Lots of them you'd never even suspect you could become a Doctor of. Like cheese – but only the stinky, blue kind.'

Green made another note.

'So you've not seen the faces, then?' asked the Doctor. 'No, of course you haven't. Limited imagination, no psychic resonance. You two wouldn't see the faces if they, well... stared you in the face. Listen to me carefully: I have to get back to the hospital.'

'You going nowhere,' said Grey. 'Not while you're being questioned on suspicion of murder.'

'I didn't murder anyone!' cried the Doctor. 'It was your officer who severed the link between Ben and the Shroud.'

Green scribbled in his notebook. 'The Shroud?'

'The alien!' said the Doctor. 'The woman holding Ben's hand.'

'We do have two females in custody,' said Green, flicking back through his notes. 'A Miss Mae Callon and a Miss Clara Oswald.' He looked up at the Doctor. 'Are you saying one of these two women killed Mr Parsons?'

'No, of course not,' replied the Doctor. 'It was the other woman. The one with the dog's eyes.'

Green checked his paperwork again. 'The arresting officer said he initially thought there were three women present at the murder scene,' he said to his colleague, 'but he later corrected that figure down to two. There is no mention of a woman "with dog's eyes".'

The Doctor sighed. 'That's because she disappeared as soon as your officer pulled Ben away from her. He was already dead. She couldn't feed on his grief any longer…' He gasped, his eyes wide. 'Of course! Don't you see? It's the Kübler-Ross model! She was right!'

Green looked confused. 'Kübler who?'

'Elisabeth Kübler-Ross,' cried the Doctor. 'She posited there were five stages of grief – denial, anger, bargaining, depression and acceptance. I argued with her at the time, but she was right. It's all in the book she published in 1969.'

'1969?' queried Grey. 'You do realise this is 1963?'

'Yes, sorry,' said the Doctor. 'It's in the book she's *going* to publish in 1969. It fits perfectly. Ben kept saying it couldn't be happening. He was in denial.

The longer people stay connected to the Shroud, the further they'll progress – and when they reach acceptance…' He reached across the table to snatch Green's notepad and pen, then began to scribble out equations at a furious rate.

Green watched him work for a second, then leaned forward. 'Sir, please don't take offence, but have you ever been a resident of an institution of any kind?'

'For a little while,' said the Doctor without looking up from his calculations. 'It was Bedlam.'

'You mean it was a chaotic place?' said Green. 'Badly run? Is that how you managed to escape?'

'What? No. It was *called* Bedlam,' said the Doctor. 'I spent my gap year there. Nice place once you got used to all the wailing and gnashing of teeth. Good gruel, too, if I recall. Of course, it had gone downhill by the time I went to visit Peter Streete there after he'd gone mad designing the Globe theatre.' He finished his work and sat back, a look of horror on his face. 'Eleven hours.'

Grey shared another glance with his colleague. 'Sir?'

The Doctor jumped to his feet again and began to pace back and forth. 'The Shroud aren't just feeding on the grief – they're cultivating it. Sowing the seeds for their own nourishment. The epicentre is here in Dallas, because of President Kennedy's assassination – but it will spread to the rest of the planet within eleven hours, and if the human race reaches the acceptance stage before I can find a way to stop the attack, there'll be no way to reverse it.'

'This is connected to the death of the President?' asked Grey.

'Of course it is!' cried the Doctor. 'That's the event the Shroud were waiting for. Oh, if only Jack was here now. He'd tell you to listen to me.'

'Are you saying you knew President Kennedy?'

'Yes, well – no. Sort of. I met him back in the 1950s, just before I accidentally got engaged to Marilyn Monroe at Frank Sinatra's house.'

Green dropped his notebook onto the table and rubbed his forehead with his hand. 'I'm getting a headache.'

The Doctor strode over to a mirror filling one entire wall of the interview room and banged on the glass. 'Hello? I know this is a two-way mirror, and there's someone on the other side of it. You in there – I have to talk to you.' There was no response. He sighed. 'Believe me, we really don't have the time for this. If you won't come out, I'll just have to clear the glass,' he warned. He reached into his jacket pocket, then sighed again. 'Did you really have to confiscate my screwdriver?' he asked, turning to Grey and Green.

'Screwdriver? What are you talking about?' demanded Grey.

The Doctor turned back to the mirror. 'Whoever

you are, you're the one in charge,' he said. 'So please get Abbott and Costello out of here and let me speak to someone who hasn't got the imagination of a piece of toast!'

The door opened and an older man in an ill-fitting chequered suit entered the room. The Doctor looked up at him with a smile. 'If you lot were doing this properly, he'd be about to tell us that he's just one day away from retirement, and that he's getting too old for this poop.'

The new arrival ignored the Doctor's comment. 'I'll take it from here,' he told the detectives.

'On whose authority?' demanded Green.

The man in the bad suit flipped open his wallet to reveal a gold badge inside. 'FBI,' he said flatly.

Grumbling, Grey and Green collected up their notes and marched out of the room, slamming the door behind them. The older man took one of the now vacant chairs.

The Doctor smiled. 'The man behind the mirror, I presume.'

'My name is Special Agent Warren Skeet,' said the man, folding his arms. 'Tell me about the Shroud.'

The Doctor sat forward. 'You believe me?'

'I didn't say that.'

'You don't have to,' said the Doctor. 'I can tell from the look in your eyes.' He sat forward. 'Who did you see?'

'My partner,' said Warren. 'Jock.'

'But Jock is dead,' said the Doctor. 'Am I right?'

Warren remained silent.

'How did you get away from Jock?'

'His face was on a window pane,' said Warren. 'I smashed it. He said some things…'

'Then you're one of the lucky ones,' said the Doctor.

'Can you help the people who have seen the faces?'

'Not from here, I can't.'

'Letting you out could cost me my job.'

'Keeping me here could cost you your planet.'

Warren took a deep breath, then pulled a coin from his pocket. He flipped it. 'Tails,' he said. 'You're free to go.' He produced the sonic screwdriver from his pocket and slid it across the table. 'What do you need from me?'

The Doctor snatched up the sonic, spun it and slipped it inside his jacket. 'First, you can let my friends out,' he said. 'And then I need to get back to the hospital. That's where the biggest concentration of faces is.'

'I wasn't enjoying this career anyway,' said Warren, pushing his chair back and standing up. 'Let's go.' He pulled open the door, the Doctor at his heels – then they both stopped suddenly.

Green suit was standing right outside the door, holding hands with a woman in a blue veil. He was muttering, just like Ben. 'This isn't happening. It can't be happening.'

'Don't touch them!' said the Doctor, pulling Warren back. 'Either of them.' He stepped out into the corridor, pressing his back against the wall to avoid accidentally rubbing against Green.

'What's happened to him?'

'It's the faces,' said the Doctor. 'The Shroud. This is what happens when they finally push through.'

'Can you help him?' asked Warren. 'Get him away from her?'

The Doctor ran his sonic up and down Green's body, then over the hand through which he was connected to the alien. 'I'm sorry,' he said, checking the readings. 'He's been in there for several minutes. If I try to break the link, he'll die just like Ben Parsons did.'

'Well, we can't just leave him like that!'

'We have to,' said the Doctor. He pocketed his sonic. 'What's his name?'

'Michael,' said Warren. 'Detective Michael Green.'

The Doctor smiled, despite himself. 'Well, I wasn't expecting to hear that,' he said. 'Actually, I can't hear anything at all.' He took half a dozen steps along the corridor, then paused to listen. 'This is the headquarters of the Dallas Police Department, but it's silent. No phones, no talking, no footsteps.' He spun back to face Warren. 'Come on!'

They discovered Grey holding hands with one of the Shroud in the cafeteria, tears silently rolling down his cheeks. And he wasn't alone. The room was filled with police officers, detectives and civilians, all connected to blue-veiled women. All except a girl in her teens they found cowering beside a refrigerator in the kitchen area. She screamed and tried to force herself further back into the tiny cubby hole at the sight of the two men.

'Hello,' said the Doctor kindly. 'I'm the Doctor and this is Warren. There's no need to be scared of us.'

The girl looked quickly from the Doctor to the FBI agent and back again, her eyes filled with fear.

The Doctor took her trembling hand in his. 'What's your name?'

'P-Peggy,' the girl stammered.

'OK, Peggy,' he said, pulling his psychic paper from his pocket. 'I need you to read to me what it says on here…'

Peggy glanced at the paper, then looked back up at the Doctor. 'It doesn't say anything,' she whimpered.

'As I thought,' said the Doctor to Warren, closing the wallet and slipping it away. 'Low psychic resonance. She won't have seen a face.'

'Does that mean she's safe?' Warren asked.

'For now,' replied the Doctor. 'Peggy,' he said, turning his attention back to the girl. 'There's a drill going on, a kind of emergency exercise…'

Peggy frowned through her tears. 'You mean this

isn't real?'

'Of course not,' beamed the Doctor. 'It's just one of those "duck and cover" things. Boring, really, but very important in case of a real disaster.'

Peggy nodded. Wiping her eyes with the back of her hand. 'What do I have to do?'

The Doctor pulled her to her feet. 'Come with us,' he said with a smile. 'I've got a very important part in the exercise for you. I want you to play a prisoner.'

'But I ain't no actress.'

'Don't you sell yourself short,' said the Doctor. 'Not with the way you're pretending to look so scared right now. You're a star in the making.'

Peggy giggled nervously. 'You think?'

'It's like being at the movies,' said the Doctor. 'Now, if Warren will kindly lead the way to the cells, we'll get you into your role.'

A few minutes later, Peggy was sitting on a cold stone bench in a vacant police cell. 'How am I doing?' she asked.

'Perfect!' enthused the Doctor. 'Now, if you'll forgive a little direction – I want you to stay locked in here until someone comes and tells you it's safe to come out. It might take a while, mind you. And whatever you do, don't touch anyone with a blue veil over their face – they're the actresses playing infected citizens.'

'I won't!'

The Doctor and Warren backed out of the cell.

'Ready for your close-up?' the Doctor winked.

Peggy giggled again.

'… and action!'

Warren closed and locked the cell door. 'Will she be safe in there?' he asked.

'Safer than a lot of other people,' said the Doctor. 'Now, see if you can get me the keys to the other cells.'

They found Clara and Mae in a cell together at the end of the row. Clara hugged the Doctor tightly. 'I didn't know what they'd done to you,' she cried.

'I've been making new friends,' said the Doctor disentangling himself from Clara. 'Clara, Mae – meet Warren.'

Clara shook the FBI agent's hand.

'Where's Ben?' asked Mae, looking round.

'I'm so sorry,' said the Doctor.

Mae slumped back against the wall with a gasp.

'What happened?' asked Clara.

'He went into shock,' the Doctor explained. The Shroud was deep inside his mind when the link was severed. But it wasn't the police officer's fault. He wasn't to know it would have that effect.'

'Then we have to go back,' said Mae.

'He's not there any more,' said Warren. 'The coroner removed his body from the office shortly after you were all arrested.'

'I don't mean that,' said Mae. She turned to the Doctor. 'You've got a time machine – now prove it!

Go back and stop Ben from touching that thing.'

'It doesn't work like that,' said the Doctor. 'I can't.'

'But you have to—'

'I can't!' said the Doctor firmly. 'I'm so sorry.'

Mae buried her head into her hands, sobbing.

Clara hugged her. 'So what do we do, Doctor?' she asked over Mae's shoulder.

'I don't know,' the Doctor admitted, pacing again. 'Ben was beginning to reject the Shroud when the link was severed, but I can't go into every single person's memories and encourage them to do the same. We don't have the time.' He stopped pacing and turned. 'There has to be a—'

Suddenly, they heard the noise of engines, and the Doctor ran to the window, jumping onto a bench to see out. 'No, no, *no!*' he cried, darting for the door.

Warren, Mae and Clara ran out after him. Dozens of dark green military vehicles were driving past in convoy.

'I have to get back to the hospital,' said the Doctor.

Chapter 8

The ambulance screeched to a halt at the checkpoint blocking the entrance to the hospital grounds. A lorry was parked across the road behind a long coil of barbed wire.

The drive across the city had been tough. The streets were filled with scores of people holding hands with blue-veiled women, and they had been forced to drive carefully around each pairing.

The Doctor jumped out of the ambulance and raced over to the armed soldier manning the barrier. 'Hello,' he said. 'That's a lovely barricade you have there. Very well done. Listen, I know you're not supposed to let anyone through but the thing is I really, really have to speak to whoever is in charge.'

'I'm sorry, sir,' said the soldier. 'General West

has set up his command headquarters inside the hospital. No civilians allowed, unless it involves a medical emergency.'

'We're in an ambulance,' the Doctor pointed out. 'What makes you think this isn't a medical emergency?'

The soldier shrugged. 'You're not a doctor.'

'Ha! I am too a doctor, and I can prove it.' He began to rummage through his pockets.

'What's the hold-up?' called Clara from the ambulance.

'I've lost my stethoscope!' the Doctor cried, looking genuinely mournful. He turned back to the soldier. 'What's your name?'

'Private Wright, sir,' the young man replied.

'OK, Private Wright,' said the Doctor urgently. 'Here's the thing. You need to let us through this barricade of yours. The future of the entire human race could depend on it.'

'I'm afraid that really isn't possible, sir. I'm just doing my job.'

'Yes, and you're doing it very well, unfortunately,' sighed the Doctor. 'Is there anyone else here I can talk to? Anyone of a higher rank?'

'There's Sergeant Scott.'

'Marvellous, in which case – can I please speak with Sergeant Scott?'

Private Wright shrugged again. 'Sarge!' he called out, stepping back to look behind the lorry. 'There's someone here who—' Suddenly, he raised his rifle and aimed at someone or something the Doctor was unable to see. 'Ma'am – step away this instant!'

The Doctor leapt over the coil of barbed wire and hurried to Private Wright's side. Behind the lorry, another soldier – Sergeant Scott by the insignia on his uniform – was holding hands with a woman in a blue veil and matching dress. Tears were rolling down the sergeant's cheeks and he was muttering to himself. 'This isn't real. It can't be real.'

'I said step away from the sergeant now!' yelled Private Wright. 'Sarge! Sarge! Can you hear me?'

Sergeant Scott continued to cry and moan.

The Doctor rested a hand on the young soldier's shoulder. 'I'm so sorry,' he said. 'There's nothing I can do right now to help him, but if you let us through I might be able to find a way.'

Private Wright shrugged off the Doctor's hand and took a step towards the silent woman, his gun still aiming at her. 'This is your final warning, ma'am!' he shouted. 'Release the sergeant's hand immediately or I will open fire!'

'Don't!' warned the Doctor. 'She's not what you think she is…'

Private Wright spun on the Doctor, finger twitching on the trigger. 'Then tell me what she is, sir!'

'I can't,' said the Doctor, 'not in a way you would understand right now.' He held his hands out. 'Give me the gun, and we can talk—'

'No, don't!' Sergeant Scott fell to his knees, lost in his memories. 'No!'

The woman dropped to her knees beside him.

Private Wright turned the gun on her again. 'Step away from my sergeant!'

'Soldier!' said the Doctor firmly. 'Lower your weapon. Please.'

The terrified private briefly turned his gun on the Doctor, then back to the woman clutching his sergeant's hand. He was blinking back tears of his own. 'I don't… I don't…'

'You don't understand,' said the Doctor, finishing the young man's sentence. 'That's fine. Really it is. But you have to listen to me. I can help…'

Then Sergeant Scott threw back his head and wailed like an injured animal.

Crack!

Private Wright fired his rifle. A bullet hole appeared briefly in the centre of the Shroud's chest, then the creature vanished in a shower of blue sparks. Instantly, Sergeant Scott fell to the ground, shaking and coughing as though in the midst of a choking fit.

The Doctor dropped to his knees beside him, his fingers feeling for a pulse in the soldier's neck. He thought he'd found it for a second but then, nothing. Sergeant Scott slumped down, unmoving.

'What happened?' cried a voice. 'We heard a

gunshot.' The Doctor looked up to find Warren standing behind him. Clara and Mae were peering around the side of the lorry.

Private Wright was frozen to the spot, his rifle still clutched in his trembling hands.

'Help Clara put the sergeant's body in the back of the truck,' the Doctor said to Warren. 'Mae, find somewhere quiet for Private Wright to sit. Then I need all of you to meet me outside the hospital.'

'What are you going to do?' asked Clara.

The Doctor stood, taking a final look at the dead soldier at his feet. 'I'm going to talk to whoever's in charge around here.'

Leaving them to their tasks, the Doctor raced across the parking lot and up the steps into the hospital reception area – only to be stopped by another armed guard.

'I'm sorry sir,' the soldier said. 'You can't go any further.'

'Here we go again,' said the Doctor to himself. 'Another bout with the military mind…' He smiled pleasantly to the guard. 'Really? No further?'

'I'm afraid not, sir. Access to the hospital is restricted to military personnel only.'

'Exactly what I was hoping you'd say!' beamed the Doctor, turning to leave. 'Thank you so much for your time.'

He found Warren, Mae and Clara waiting for him on the steps outside. 'I need a diversion,' he said quietly.

'But even if you get past this guy, there will be other soldiers inside,' said Clara. 'You won't get as far as the General.'

'I will if I go via the TARDIS first...'

A few moments later, the Doctor ducked into an alcove and watched as Warren climbed the steps to reception, breathing heavily. As he reached the top, he clutched at his chest and collapsed. Mae and Clara ran up to kneel beside him. 'Help!' cried Mae. 'I think he's had a heart attack! Someone help!

The soldier on duty dashed to their side, allowing the Doctor to slip unnoticed down the corridor behind him.

General Harley B. West spread his map of Dallas over the surface of the table and stood back to admire his work. In less than an hour, he had transformed one of the hospital's operating theatres into a command centre for the Texas National Guard. Of course, several patients had been forced to have their operations postponed as a result, but there were always going to be casualties when the might of the military was brought in to defend the greatest nation in the world.

As soon as he had heard about the strange faces appearing all over the city, General West had put his unit on standby. Thankfully, they were still in a state of readiness since yesterday. After hearing of President Kennedy's assassination, General West had prepared his troops to enforce the state of martial law he imagined would be instigated in the area. Instead, the powers that be had simply cordoned off Dealey Plaza as though it were a common or garden crime scene and not an assault on democracy itself. OK, maybe he hadn't been a supporter of this particular President, but he would fight to his last breath to defend the freedoms that had allowed the man to be voted into office.

This wasn't the first time the state governors had ignored his advice, either. There was that sorry business last year when the Soviets had stationed missiles in Cuba and threatened to launch them at the USA. Just thinking about it made the General's blood boil and he was forced to grip the edge of the operating table to control his rage. Of course, he'd been one of the few voices calling for an all-out tactical strike on Cuba for agreeing to side with Moscow. Castro couldn't fire missiles from the bottom of the sea, he'd pointed out. However, democracy and negotiation had triumphed in the end. Another war – and another chance for General West to be bathed in military glory – had been averted.

Still, he had to stay positive. He'd get his ticker-tape parade one day, and maybe this crazy, faces-out-of-nowhere nonsense was how it was going to happen. It was probably down to the Russians – as usual – and this time, those pencil pushers at the

State Capitol would be forced to listen to reason. The time for talking to those who hated freedom was over. What was needed now was swift military action, and he was just the man to provide it.

The door to the theatre swung open and his second in command, Captain Adam Keating, entered, carrying a canvas bag. He was a much younger man than the General, having progressed swiftly through the ranks due to having the steadfast support of the men he commanded and the respect of his superiors alike. Still, he wasn't all bad, and the General suspected he could hold his own in a battle, if he ever got to see one.

'Did you get them?' the General asked, smoothing the creases from his map.

'I did,' replied Keating, 'but the nurses in the children's ward weren't happy about it.'

'This is war, Keating!' snapped the General. 'We're not here to make people happy.'

'Technically, this isn't war, sir,' Keating pointed out. 'We don't know who or what we're up against yet, so we can't declare war.'

'Only a matter of time,' the old soldier grunted. 'Well? Let's see 'em.'

With a barely concealed sigh, Captain Keating tipped the contents of the bag onto the table. The General found himself faced with dozens of plastic dolls. 'Excellent work!' he exclaimed, snatching up the largest of the toys. He held it in his hands for a second, then ripped the head off and tossed the rest into the corner of the room.

'The greatest concentration of heads and faces rising up has been here at the hospital,' he said, placing the doll's head on the map. 'So we'll use that one for here...' He grabbed another doll and quickly decapitated it. 'We've also had sightings at Fair Park, Cotton Bowl Stadium and several at the Museum of Contemporary Art – although if you spend your days staring at half-naked sculptures, you deserve everything you get.'

Captain Keating watched as the General gradually covered the map with severed doll's heads. 'Do you have a plan of attack, sir?' he asked.

'Of course!' cried the General. 'We blast 'em back to Russia, where they came from!'

'If you will pardon me, sir,' Keating put in. 'We don't know they're from Russia. Can I suggest we study the enemy for a while longer before we begin blasting them?'

'Very wise, what what!' barked a voice from the doorway before the General could reply. Keating turned to find a tall, thin man in British military uniform crossing the room. His hair (almost certainly longer than any army allowed) was plastered to his head with oil, and he wore a dark moustache which sloped ever so slightly down to the left.

The General's hand hovered over the handle of his service pistol. 'Now, just who in the name of tarnation are you?' he demanded.

'The name's Lethbridge-Stewart!' announced the newcomer. 'Brigadier Alistair Gord— No, wait, hang on... it's still 1963, isn't it?' He stopped to count on his fingers for a moment. 'Right, yes! I'm *Colonel* Alistair Gordon Lethbridge-Stewart. British army, old bean! Delighted to meet you, what!' He held out a hand, which the General ignored.

'What are you doing here?' the Texan drawled.

'Been drafted in to help with these pesky heads,' said the Brit. 'Sort the blighters out once and for all. Greyhound Leader to Trap One, and all that, my old mucker.'

'Drafted in?' said the General. 'By who?'

Colonel Lethbridge-Stewart's eyes flicked as he appeared to think. 'Why, the Pentagon, old chap!' he said after a second or two. 'I've been over here, working on a couple of military-style projects – you know, stuff with soldiers and the like – and as soon as they heard about all these blinking faces, they put me on the first flight down here. Or up here. Whichever direction it is.' He reached up to his collar to adjust his tie, then seemed to change his mind at the last moment and instead twirled the ends of his moustache.

The General's eyes narrowed. 'You've seen these things before?'

'Not exactly like these, skipper,' replied the Colonel. 'But situations like this are right up my bloomin' street, old fellow. I'd listen carefully and do exactly as I say, if I were you.'

The General snarled. 'The Pentagon may have sent some lily-livered Limey down to offer advice, but I'm still in charge around here, get it?'

'Of course, old sport,' blurted out Lethbridge-Stewart. He unholstered his own gun and waved it carelessly in the air. 'Now, who do I have to shoot to get a cup of tea around here?'

Captain Keating ducked below the line of the barrel. 'Er, I'll be happy to get you some tea, sir,' he said, 'if you could just secure your weapon?'

'Certainly, old fellow!' beamed the Colonel. 'Never much liked these things, anyway.' He slid his pistol back in its holster on the third attempt, and Keating left the room. 'Now, then...' he said, leaning over the doll head-festooned map. 'What do we have here?'

'An up-to-the-minute record of faces and heads,' said the General. He didn't like having to share information with this tea-supping Brit but, if the Pentagon had sent him to help out, he would be filing a report back. He'd play along and include the fool – for the time being. 'I need to know exactly where they are so I can wipe 'em off the face of the Earth.' The General laughed heartily, and slapped Lethbridge-Stewart on the back. When he was able to breathe again, the Colonel joined in with the guffaws.

'Top whizz, what what!' Lethbridge-Stewart exclaimed. 'But what about the element of surprise?'

'What about it?'

'Well, think about it, old man… If you go in all guns blazing, word could spread among the enemy that they're under attack. However, if you position your troops out of sight of the blighters, you can spring the trap when the time is right!'

A smile crept across the General's face. 'Catch 'em unawares, you mean?'

'That's the idea!'

General West turned and paced across the room and back, mulling the idea over in his mind. 'I guess that would mean I could put a stop to the invasion in one fell swoop…'

'Invasion?' said the Colonel. 'You know it's an invasion?'

'Well, of course it is!' the General cried. 'A commie invasion!'

'Oh, er… yes. Of course!'

'And putting a stop to an entire invasion with a single command… Now, that would get me noticed!'

'You bet it would!' said Lethbridge-Stewart, clapping his hand on the General's back. He spotted the old soldier's reaction and quickly stuffed his hand into his jacket pocket. 'I should imagine it would impress a lot of the big cheeses back in Washington.'

The General grinned. As crazy as this British

guy was, he liked the sound of being noticed by the big cheeses, whatever they were. 'So where would you suggest I station my troops? Out of sight of the enemy?'

'Completely out of sight!' said the Colonel. He pulled his hand out of his pocket and opened it to reveal a dozen or so candies shaped like little men. 'In fact, if I were you, I'd take them right back to here.' He dropped the sweets onto an area near the outer edge of the map.

The General leaned in to examine the area and scowled. 'That's my barracks,' he said flatly.

'Precisely, old chap,' enthused Lethbridge-Stewart. 'And that's exactly what those no-good Johnnies wouldn't expect you to do.'

'But it's a complete withdrawal of my men!'

Colonel Lethbridge-Stewart wagged a long finger in the air. 'That may be what it looks like, old sport,' he agreed. 'But in reality, it's a shrewd military tactic.'

The door swung open and Captain Keating returned, carrying a tray of cups. 'Spiffing!' cried the Colonel. 'I'm bloomin' parched, squire!'

But instead of offering tea, Keating spun around and pointed a gun at the British officer. 'You're an impostor!' he snarled. 'Put your hands in the air!'

'Gosh!' exclaimed Colonel Lethbridge-Stewart, raising his arms. 'I'll have the coffee if tea is this much trouble.'

'The coffee is for the General,' snarled Keating. 'I'm sorry I took so long making it, sir – I made a telephone call while I was away. A telephone call to British military headquarters, who told me that the *real* Colonel Lethbridge-Stewart is currently on tactical manoeuvres on Salisbury Plain.'

'What?' roared General West. 'Are you saying this man isn't the real thing?'

'That's exactly what I'm saying,' said Keating, reaching for the British soldier's fake moustache. Lethbridge-Stewart leaned back to try to keep the facial hair out of his grasp, but the Captain simply lunged forward and ripped it off.

'Ow!' cried the counterfeit Colonel, clutching at his upper lip. Then he scuffed up his oiled back hair into an alarming mess. 'Hello! I'm the Doctor. I suppose the tea is out of the question now?'

'I think you've got some explaining to do,' barked the General, his own pistol now pointing at the Doctor. 'What are you doing in my command centre?'

'Yes, now that I can explain,' said the Doctor. 'Sorry about the disguise – but it was good, though, wasn't it? I needed to find a way to speak to you. General, whatever you do, you absolutely must not attack the Shroud.'

'The what?' demanded the General.

'The Shroud,' said the Doctor. 'Bit of a long story, but they're an alien race who are here to feast on the grief of human beings. I can find a way to stop them – I just need time.'

'You'll have plenty of time where you're going,' said the General, gesturing to the door with his gun. 'Captain Keating – take him away.'

'I'm being serious – you have to listen to me!'

'I'm not listening to a madman with a fake moustache. Get him out of here!'

'There's nothing wrong with a fake moustache, you know,' mumbled the Doctor as Keating ushered him out. 'You don't think Clark Gable's was real, do you? He was nobody until I stuck that 'tache on him…'

General West chose a cup from the tray and sipped at his coffee as the phony British officer was ushered out of command headquarters. 'Of all the nerve!'

Outside in the corridor, Keating turned to the Doctor. 'You know what's going on here?' he asked.

The Doctor nodded. 'A little.'

'Come with me,' said the Captain.

'You're not going anywhere,' said a voice. Captain Keating turned to find a gun aimed at his own head.

'Warren!' cried the Doctor. 'What do you think you're doing?'

'Most likely, I'm handing in my resignation,' the FBI agent replied with a grim smile. He flicked the safety catch off his pistol and called into a side room. 'I've got him.'

Clara appeared in the entrance to the room. 'Bring him in,' she ordered.

'I really don't think that's a good idea...' began the Doctor, but he was ignored. Warren led Captain Keating into the room and told him to lie down on an empty bed.

'You don't understand,' growled Keating. 'I want to help you.'

'Then lie still like a good boy,' hissed Clara as she strapped the Captain down. 'This is the recovery room, where they bring patients after their operations. They have to be secured in case they fall out of bed.'

'This isn't the way it was supposed to happen,' protested the Doctor but, once again, no one seemed to be listening.

'Any luck?' Clara called out loud.

Mae appeared from a store cupboard at the back of the room, her hands full of small glass bottles. 'There's plenty of medication,' she said. 'But nothing that appears to be a sedative.'

'Sedative?' repeated the Doctor, rubbing his brow. 'And you need sedative to...'

'To stop him from calling out for help,' said Warren, matter-of-factly.

The Doctor sat heavily in a chair. 'This isn't good,' he muttered. 'This isn't good at all.'

'There isn't any sedative left,' said Captain Keating. 'I put it all in the General's coffee!'

Crash!

The Doctor leapt to his feet and ran back to the operating theatre. Inside, he found General Harley B. West slumped, unconscious, over his map. Doll heads were scattered all over the floor.

He returned to the recovery room, eyeing Keating warily. 'You drugged your superior officer?'

'Of course I did!' snapped Keating. 'You met the man – he's insane. Desperate for a fight. I may not have his years of experience, but I know you don't charge in and attack an opponent until you know what you're up against.'

'So why did you expose me?' asked the Doctor.

'I didn't know who you really were,' said Keating. 'Other than that you definitely weren't a genuine soldier. I couldn't risk you springing whatever plan you had in mind the second the General collapsed.'

A grin split the Doctor's face. 'Sedative,' he grinned, tapping Keating cheerily on the cheek. 'Marvellous.' He quickly began to undo the straps holding the Captain down.

'You said you can find a way to stop these things,' said Keating, sitting on the edge of the bed. 'Is that true?'

The Doctor nodded. 'I think so, yes. But we haven't got much time.'

'OK,' said Keating, taking the Doctor's hand and shaking it. 'Then I'll keep the General out of action for as long as I can. The rest is up to you.'

Chapter 9

'We're doing what?' demanded Clara, catching up as the Doctor strode along a hospital corridor. Warren and Mae hurried to keep pace with the pair of them.

'We're going back,' replied the Doctor. 'Just like Mae suggested earlier. Sorry,' he called over his shoulder. 'I should have listened to you.'

'But you said we can't go back along Ben's timeline,' Mae pointed out.

'We can't,' said the Doctor. 'Which is just as well, as we're not following Ben's timeline. We're following the Shroud's.'

Clara grabbed the Doctor's arm and stopped him. 'Now you're really not making sense,' she said.

'I'm making perfect sense,' the Doctor insisted. 'It's not my fault if you can't understand.'

'OK, then,' said Clara. 'For the benefit of us slower folk, can you please explain what we're about to do.'

The Doctor took a deep breath. 'I've never encountered the Shroud before,' he said, 'and – as much as it pains me to say this – I don't know how to stop them. So we have to go back.'

'Back where?' asked Warren.

'To the last planet the Shroud attacked,' the Doctor said. 'I'm not exactly sure where, or when, that planet is, but a quick visit might give us a clue as to what their weakness is. Help us find a way to defeat them.'

'Hang on,' said Clara. 'The TARDIS won't even take off at the moment, let alone travel to another planet. How are we going to get there?'

'The same way the Shroud got here,' said the Doctor. 'Through that wormhole, the end of which is currently surrounding the entire planet.' With that, he marched away again.

'If we're not taking the TARDIS, why are you heading over there?' Clara asked after him.

'To get out of this ridiculous outfit!' the Doctor called over his shoulder. 'I'm about to do something very clever and a tiny bit against the rules of the universe. It's important that I'm properly dressed.'

'That's a shame,' said Clara with a wink to Mae. 'I love a man in uniform.'

'I heard that!' shouted the Doctor. 'Meet me outside in five minutes. And no peeking.'

By the time Clara, Mae and Warren reached the parking lot at the front of the hospital, the Doctor was already there, back in his frock coat and black jeans and bow tie. He was examining the front wall of the building with his sonic screwdriver.

'How do you do that?' asked Clara. 'How do you get changed so quickly?'

'Wibbly-wobbly wardrobe,' said the Doctor with a sniff. 'Now, this wall leads directly into the wormhole. Well, the whole planet does in fact. But this is where we'll be going in. Any questions?'

Warren raised his hand. 'Yes, actually,' he said. 'What in God's name are you talking about?'

'Oh yes,' said the Doctor. 'I keep forgetting you weren't here from the start. Give me your sock.'

'Excuse me?'

'One of your socks,' repeated the Doctor. 'Give it to me. It'll make everything much clearer.'

Shrugging, Warren kicked off a shoe and pulled off his sock. The Doctor took it and examined the red and blue diamond pattern in the material.

'Ooh, argyle!' he exclaimed. 'I like those!' He lifted up his ankle and laid the sock against it as though trying it for size. 'Marvellous!' He turned to Clara. 'Make a note – after all this is over, we have to go shopping for argyle socks.'

Clara folded her arms. 'Watch how quickly I write that down,' she said flatly.

'I still don't get what this has to do with the

Shroud and other planets,' said Warren, slipping his shoe back onto his bare foot.

'You will in a moment,' the Doctor promised. 'Now, watch...' And with that, he pulled a pair of scissors from his pocket and cut the foot off the sock.

'Hey!' cried Warren. 'They're new!'

'They're still new,' said the Doctor. 'But now, they're educational as well...' He slipped the scissors away and pulled out a satsuma. 'OK,' he said. 'Imagine this satsuma is the Earth, sitting all alone near one end of the solar system, minding its own business.' He handed the piece of fruit to Mae, and instructed her to hold it up in the air.

'And this,' the Doctor continued, producing a nectarine from a different pocket, 'is the planet the Shroud are currently on. But they want to get off this world, and get to Earth in time for dinner.' He gave Clara the nectarine, which she also held in the air. The Doctor pulled a length of string from his trouser pocket and stretched it between the two.

'To get from one planet to another in a straight line takes a colossal amount of energy, incredibly advanced technology and more logistical organisation than every personal assistant and secretary in the world, rolled into one. Ten thousand times that if you have to cross time as well.' The Doctor ran his finger along the string from the nectarine to the satsuma. 'But...'

Grabbing the centre of the string, he began to bend

it in half, and moved Clara so that she was standing next to Mae. 'You can cheat by using something called a wormhole.'

'And that's my sock?' asked Warren.

'Exactly!' said the Doctor, slipping one end of the argyle patterned tube over the nectarine and the other end over the satsuma. 'Think of it like a short cut through space and time. A quick way to travel vast distances without all the hassle.'

'So is that how the TARDIS travels through time and space?' asked Clara.

'Sort of, yes,' said the Doctor. 'Well, no actually. The TARDIS travels through the Vortex, which is – in layman's terms – a huge, complicated, multidimensional, trans-temporal… thingy. And like Warren's sock, it comes in two lovely colours.'

'Well, I'm glad we got that cleared up,' said Clara.

The Doctor whipped out his sonic again and went back to scanning the wall beside the hospital entrance. 'So now you know what a wormhole is,' he said. 'You can keep the fruit, by the way.'

Clara and Mae smiled and pocketed their treats. Warren took what was left of his sock back, scowled at it and dumped it in a nearby bin.

'The wormhole surrounds the entire world,' said the Doctor. 'But this hospital is a weak point – lots of grief played out on a daily basis and yesterday in particular – so it will be the easiest spot to breach. All I have to do is find the right frequency to reverse the polarity of the neutron flow...' He flicked from one sonic setting to the next until, suddenly, the wall began to shimmer, as though a vertical expanse of water.

'Amazing!' breathed Clara, stepping towards the entrance of the wormhole, arm outstretched. The Doctor quickly slapped it away. 'Ow!' she cried. 'What did you do that for?'

'You were about to stick your hand through into another world!' the Doctor said. 'Apart from the fact that the wormhole is likely to vaporise human flesh and zap your fingers into a billion different directions – you don't know what's on the other side if your hand does make it intact. You could be reaching into somebody's bathroom, and that's not very good manners.'

Clara pulled her hand back, scowling. 'So how do we get through this thing if it will vaporise us on contact?'

'We use a vehicle,' explained the Doctor. 'The metal frame will act like a faraday cage, absorbing all the zappy bits and keeping the gooey stuff inside safe from harm.' Then he added: 'We're the gooey bits.'

'So, back to the ambulance then?' said Mae.

'Bingo!'

They ran across the parking lot to where they had left the ambulance earlier, and were climbing in when the Doctor spotted something in a small clump of trees that separated the hospital grounds from the main road. 'Oh, no…' he said, and hurried over.

Dr Mairi Ellison was sitting beneath one of the trees, her cheeks wet with tears. She was holding hands with one of the Shroud. The Doctor approached and made to lift the woman's veil, only for Dr Ellison to turn and glare at him.

'Get it away from me now!' she screeched. 'Get it away!'

'The anger stage,' said the Doctor, sadly. 'The Shroud's grip is intensifying. I will get it away from you Mairi, you just have to trust me.' He reached over and carefully lifted the woman's blue veil to reveal the eyes of an elderly man.

'It could be her father, perhaps,' suggested a voice. The Doctor looked up to find Clara standing behind him. He let the veil drop.

'Come on,' he said, turning to stride back towards the ambulance. He climbed into the driver's seat and fastened his seatbelt. 'Let's do this,' he said, firing up the engine with his sonic.

'Wait a minute,' said Warren, leaning through from the back section of the ambulance and resting a hand on the Doctor's shoulder. 'We're seriously about to leave Earth and go to another planet?'

The Doctor beamed. 'Yep!'

'And we'll be able to breathe there? It'll have oxygen?'

Clara and Mae turned to the Doctor in alarm.

'I was hoping nobody would think to ask that,' said the Doctor. 'But you did, Warren. Well done. Go to the top of the class and have a gold star in putting the shivers up everyone.'

'So?' said Clara. 'What's the answer? Will we be able to breathe?'

'Almost certainly,' replied the Doctor. 'Make that probably. A strong probably.'

'How can you possibly know?'

'Away from the mental tentacle thing, the Shroud have a basic humanoid biology,' the Doctor explained. 'That means they'll need the same sort of atmosphere as we do.'

'You're guessing, aren't you?'

'Have been since we got here,' said the Doctor. 'But don't let that put you off. I'm sure there's a plan forming in my head somewhere. It's bound to let me know when it's ready. Now, if nobody has any further questions, I suggest we drive at full pelt into that brick wall over there and hope we come out the other side on an alien planet.'

Revving the engine, the Doctor stamped down on the accelerator and drove at the shimmering wall. Everyone in the ambulance closed their eyes and found something to grip on to.'

'*Geronimo!*'

They emerged inside a long tunnel that looked as though it was made of solid, grey thunderclouds.

Like concrete that had been disturbed before it could set properly. The Doctor brought the ambulance to a halt, switched on the headlights and whistled appreciatively.

'Wow!' he said. 'That is new.'

'What is?' asked Mae.

'The wormhole,' said the Doctor. 'It's like nothing I've ever seen before.'

'Yeah, cos usually you've seen one wormhole, you've seen them all,' said Clara.

'Precisely,' said the Doctor, missing the sarcastic tone. 'I've not been through that many, but they've always been instantaneous before. Arrive at the other end at the exact moment you pass through – but this is incredible.'

He reached for the door handle, only for Clara to stop him. 'What are you doing?'

'Going outside for a better look,' said the Doctor.

'But you'll let all the air out!'

The Doctor's eyes narrowed. 'We're in an ambulance,' he said. 'It's not airtight. Air started getting out the second we arrived. As we're not rolling around with skin the colour of the TARDIS, I'd say there's air seeping in as well.' Then he opened the door and hopped out.

Warren and Mae climbed out of the back of the ambulance and, after a few seconds of pouting, Clara joined the group.

'It's tricky to walk,' said Warren. 'Uneven

underfoot.'

The Doctor stooped to run his fingers over the ground. 'It looks like the Vortex,' he said. 'Only dead.'

'Maybe this is what happens to wormholes after they die?' suggested Clara.

The Doctor shook his head. 'They can't die,' he said. 'They're not alive to begin with. They're just passageways. Tunnels from one time and place to another.' He pulled out a pair of ornate opera glasses and peered down the wormhole through them. 'And can you see? There's a light at the other end.'

He passed the glasses to Warren.

'I can see it,' he said. 'It's shimmering – just like the wall of the hospital was.'

'Then that must be where it comes out,' said Mae. 'The exit.'

'But it can only be a couple of miles away,' said Warren, handing the opera glasses back to the Doctor. 'Not even as far as the Moon.'

'You're forgetting,' said the Doctor. 'The actual wormhole may only be a few miles long, but it may cover several thousand light years, or even more.'

'So we've still no idea where it will take us,' said Mae.

'Only one way to find out,' said Clara, opening the driver's door for the Doctor. 'All aboard. Next stop, the mysterious world!'

They climbed back into the ambulance and

continued driving. The journey was hard going, with the Doctor having to swerve to avoid some of the larger protrusions jutting up from the tunnel floor. More than once, they heard a metallic rasp as the side of the ambulance scraped along the sides of the wormhole.

Suddenly, Mae gasped. 'Oh my God! I've just realised what those things are.'

'What things?' asked Clara.

'The things sticking out of the walls and the ground,' cried Mae. 'They look like rocks and lumps of stone, but they're not. They're bodies!'

Clara looked out of the window and clamped a hand over her mouth. Mae was right. There, protruding from the grey rock was a shoulder and the back of a head.

The Doctor sighed. 'Warren,' he said. 'You'll have to hand over your "putting the shivers up other people" crown, I'm afraid. We have a new champion.'

Clara spun in her seat to face him. 'You knew they were bodies?'

'I've been to Pompeii,' the Doctor said. 'Both on the big day itself, and again years later. The figures covered in ash from Mount Vesuvius looked a lot like these poor folk.'

'But who are they?' asked Mae. 'I mean, who were they?'

The Doctor took a moment to choose his words.

'They're victims of the Shroud,' he said eventually. 'They must have brought some people from their previous planet with them on the journey. Like a packed lunch. These are the leftovers.'

The colour drained from Mae's cheeks. 'That's terrib—'

Flash!

Suddenly, Mae was no longer sitting in the back of the ambulance with Warren. In fact, she wasn't in the ambulance – or the wormhole – at all. She was in a small, dark room, hammering on a metal door.

Flash!

Mae jumped in her seat and screamed. The Doctor hit the brake and spun round, sonic at the ready. 'What is it?' he asked.

Mae's eyes darted back and forth. Her breathing was ragged and she could feel her heart thumping in her chest. 'I… I don't know. I wasn't here. In the ambulance, I mean. I was in some kind of room, but I couldn't get out.'

The Doctor scanned her with the sonic. 'Well, you didn't physically move,' he said, checking the results. 'It must have been a mental jump of some kind. Maybe you picked up on some psychic residue left behind.'

Mae looked horrified at the suggestion. 'You mean I felt what one of those people out there went through before they… before they died?'

The Doctor nodded and continued driving. The

shimmering exit to the wormhole was clearly in sight ahead of them now. 'The closer we get to the other planet, the stronger the connection with its victims. It could be the reason the wormhole looks like an actual tunnel. It holds the remains of the Shroud's prey – both physical and as psychic energy. It can't close in on itself like it should.'

Warren reached over to take Mae's hand. 'It's OK,' he said, 'I'll make sure that—'

Flash!

Warren was running down a corridor, fighting his way against hundreds of people swarming in the opposite direction, trying to find a way through. 'Orma!' he cried. 'Orma!'

Flash!

Warren jerked back in his seat, surprised to find the others staring at him. 'What?'

'Who or what is Orma?' the Doctor asked.

'I don't know,' Warren admitted warily. 'Why?'

'You were just shouting it,' said Clara.

Warren let out a deep breath. 'It happened to me as well,' he said. 'For a second, I wasn't here in the ambulance. I was trying to force my way through a crowd of people. Everyone around me was terrified.'

'OK,' said the Doctor, turning back and shifting the engine into drive and flooring the accelerator. 'The sooner we get out of here, the better. There's a lot of psychic flotsam and jetsam floating around.' The ambulance began to judder as it bounced over the lumps in the ground. 'Just try not to think about what we're driving over.'

'But what if it's like that when we arrive on the other planet?' asked Clara. 'What if we get there and all we can—'

Flash!

Clara sat bolt upright in bed. The room was dark. Even the electro-gleam had gone out. 'Mother!' she called out. 'Mother, are you there?'

There was no reply. Nervously, Clara pulled back the thick blankets and stepped onto the smooth metal floor. It felt cold against her bare feet. She reached for the lamp that always sat on her bedside table, knowing that it wouldn't have much oil left in it – not at this stage of the season – but it should be enough to give her a few minutes of light. She found a match and struck it, trying to hold the flame steady in her trembling fingers to allow the wick to catch. After a few seconds, it began to glow and she found with relief that she was still in her own bedroom.

No, thought Clara to herself. This isn't my bedroom. My bedroom is back in London. But this room – with its painted metal walls and dressing table made from the remnants of an old travel capsule – seemed like the most familiar place of all to her.

Suddenly, there was a knock on the door. No, more than a knock. Someone had hammered on it. Who could be outside? It had to be late, perhaps even the middle of the night.

'Who's there?' Clara asked, her voice cracking. Then she froze. That wasn't her voice. She was much older than that voice sounded. Holding the lamp out in front of her, she made her way over to the dressing table and peered into the piece of polished steel that served as a mirror. Looking back at her was the face of a young girl. A girl of maybe 9 or 10 years old. Clara raised a hand to her face and touched her lips – and the girl in the mirror did the same.

Banging at the door again – only this time, the door moved. It opened inward, just a few inches, but it was enough to terrify Clara. Blowing out the lamp, she leapt into bed and pulled the blankets over her head. Maybe this was all a nightmare. Maybe if she could fall back asleep, everything would go back to normal.

The bedroom door crashed open and Clara jumped beneath her blankets. Whoever had been knocking was now inside her room. She could hear their footsteps clanking on the metal floor. They were obviously wearing boots. Then the intruder pulled back her blankets and shone a bright light in her eyes. A bright, green light. And there was a noise, too. A kind of a *Vreeeeeeeeee!*

'There you are!' said the Doctor.

Flash!

Clara jumped in her seat. She was back in the ambulance – only Warren was now driving and the Doctor was squeezed between them, his fingers pressed against her forehead.

'What are you doing?' she cried, pushing his hands away.

The Doctor looked confused for a moment. 'I was saving you.'

'You went inside my mind?'

'Yes. To save you.'

'You went inside my mind without my permission?'

'Again, you seem to be missing the "I saved you" part.'

'Don't ever do that again!'

'What? Save you?'

'No. Go in there without my permission.'

The Doctor nervously fiddled with his bow tie. 'OK,' he said.

'Unless you absolutely have to do it to save me, of course,' said Clara. Then she gasped as the memory of what she had seen hit her. 'We have to find the girl!'

'Which girl?' asked the Doctor.

'Didn't you see her?' asked Clara. 'She was... well, she was me.'

The Doctor shook his head. 'The only person I saw in that room looked like you.'

Clara sat back, clearly distressed. 'She was so alone.'

They drove in silence for a few minutes, then

Warren spoke up. 'OK, ' he said. 'End of the road, folks.' The shimmering end of the wormhole was rushing towards them.

The Doctor climbed into the rear of the ambulance with Mae and sat on the stretcher. 'Good luck, everyone,' he said, gripping onto an oxygen bottle fixed to the wall.

Then the ambulance burst through into another world.

Chapter 10

The ambulance exploded through the shimmering portal at the end of the wormhole where it landed on an expanse of ice and began to skid sideways, its wheels spinning as they desperately tried to find some traction on the slippery ground. Warren pumped at the brakes, dragging the wheel in the opposite direction to the skid in an effort to slow the vehicle's momentum. After turning in two full circles, it slammed side-on into a tall snowdrift. The engine sputtered and died.

'Anyone hurt?' called the Doctor, finally releasing his grip on the sides of the stretcher. Mae, Clara and Warren confirmed that they were all fine.

'Good,' said the Doctor, leaning between the front seats to peer through the window. Outside, everything was brilliant white and, apart from the driving rain hammering down on the roof of the vehicle, completely silent.

'Wherever we are, we appear to have arrived in the middle of winter,' Mae pointed out.

'Not necessarily,' said the Doctor, reaching across Clara to wind down her window. 'This could be what summer is like here. Or it could be a mixture of winter and summer running at exactly the same time.' He took a deep breath of the ice cold air. 'A brand new season called wummer.'

'Wummer?' said Clara, slapping his hand away and winding her window closed again.

The Doctor sniffed. 'Maybe not. Come on, let's find some civilisation.' He pointed his sonic screwdriver at the ignition and gave it a blast. The engine started on the fourth attempt, but the ambulance wouldn't respond to Warren's commands. The wheels simply spun on the icy ground.

'We're stuck,' he said, shifting the gears back into 'park'. 'Wedged in the snowdrift.'

'Then we'll have to dig our way out,' said the Doctor. He flung the back doors of the ambulance open and leapt out, immediately losing his footing and landing hard on his bottom. 'Watch out for that first step,' he cried as he hauled himself to his feet. 'It's a doozy!'

Clara and Mae joined him, shivering against the freezing rain. 'Where do we start?' asked Mae. But the Doctor didn't answer. He was studying the area around them with interest.

'Look,' he said, pointing to the far end of the snowdrift they had hit. 'A row of houses.'

'They're tiny,' said Clara. 'There's not one of them over a single storey high.'

'It looks like they're built into the side of the hill,' said the Doctor.

'Like hobbit holes,' said Clara.

'Exactly like hobbit holes!' agreed the Doctor.

'So we've come to the planet of the little people?'

'Not necessarily,' said the Doctor. 'The doorways look around average human height from here. And have you noticed that some of them are hanging off their hinges?'

Clara squinted to get a better view through the lashing rain. 'A lot of the windows are broken, too,' she said. 'I wonder why?'

'I've no idea,' said the Doctor. 'But I'd be very interested to find out.'

Mae wrapped her arms around herself. 'Can we examine the local architecture *after* we've dug the ambulance out of the snow and got back in the warm, do you think?'

'Of course,' grinned the Doctor. 'We just need something to dig with.'

There was a crack of wood, and Warren appeared, holding the decorative panel from the inside of the driver's door. 'We could use these,' he suggested.

'We're already in trouble for stealing the ambulance,' Clara reminded him. 'I'm not sure we should start vandalising it as well.'

'If you'd prefer us to dig with our hands, that's fine,' said Warren. 'But it's likely to take at least twice as long, and we could end up losing our fingers to frostbite…'

'Give me that!' said Clara with a smirk, snatching the piece of wood.

Warren chuckled and went back to break off some more panelling.

It took them around twenty minutes to free the side of the ambulance from its snowy tomb, by which time they were all soaking wet and shivering with cold. Warren shunted the engine into drive and finally coaxed the vehicle into moving forwards, even if the wheels were still finding it difficult to grip the ground.

Clara jumped into the front passenger seat and cranked up the heating. 'I thought I'd never be warm again,' she groaned.

The Doctor leapt into the back with Mae and slammed the doors shut. He was giving Warren instructions as to which might be the best direction to drive when a group of people – very much like humans but with much paler skin and dark, round eyes – leapt over the top of the snowdrift and began to approach the ambulance, spreading out to surround it.

'Hello!' said the Doctor, cheerily. 'Looks like the welcoming committee have spotted us.'

'They don't look very welcoming to me,' Clara pointed out.

'Give them a chance,' said the Doctor. 'This might be their way of greeting strangers...'

The people edged closer to the ambulance, arms outstretched. They were all dressed in ragged clothes and wrapped in old blankets. Their faces and hands were covered in scabs and sores. A woman with sunken cheeks stared through the windscreen at the occupants of the ambulance and spat angrily, baring blackened, broken teeth.

The Doctor shrugged. 'Then again...'

A tall, thin man suddenly darted forward. He grabbed one of the ambulance's wing mirrors and began to wrestle with it.

Warren sounded the horn. 'Get out of here!' he shouted.

The crowd jumped back at the noise but, once they realised the sound hadn't done more than startle them, they approached again. Once more, the tall man clutched at the wing mirror and, after a moment, he tore it free.

The figure hugged the prize to his chest and turned to run away, but only managed a few steps before two of the others from the group lunged for him. They dragged him to the ground, fighting for the mirror, punching and kicking its temporary owner into submission.

'OK,' said the Doctor. 'I think we need to get away from here.'

'I was just thinking the same thing,' said Warren, shifting the engine back into 'drive'.

Before they could move, the rear doors of the ambulance were pulled open, and three more of the attackers began to climb inside. Mae screamed at the sight of them and tried to close the doors, but one of the men grabbed hold of her leg and dragged her back out onto the ice.

'Mae!' The Doctor jumped out after her, crashing down on top of her abductor and sending him sprawling. By the time he was back on his feet, two women had hold of Mae's arms and were dragging her away towards the row of hobbit houses.

'Doctor!' bellowed Clara. 'Behind you!'

There was a thump of metal, and the Doctor whirled round to see two more of the group battering on the sides of the ambulance, and a third clambering up onto the roof. 'Drive!' he yelled to Warren, slamming the back doors. 'I'm going after Mae. I'll find you!'

Nodding, Warren stamped down on the accelerator. The wheels spun crazily, then finally caught and the ambulance jerked forward. Several of the gang were forced to dive out of the way to avoid being dragged under the vehicle as it sped away.

Certain Clara and Warren were safe, the Doctor ran after Mae and her kidnappers. It was hard to see where they had gone in the driving rain, and the icy ground caused him to slip to his knees more than once. Then he caught a flash of Mae's red jumper up ahead and raced after it, stomping down hard to dig the heels of his boots into the ground with each step.

The two women were obviously more used to running in these conditions than the Doctor, but Mae was putting up quite a fight which was enough to slow them down.

'Stop where you are!' the Doctor roared, appearing out of the rain behind them. He was using his sonic as a torch, the green light illuminating the snow around him eerily. At the sight of this magical instrument, the two women seemed to forget about Mae, releasing their grip on her and allowing her to slump to the wet ground. They began to advance on the Doctor, their large eyes fixed hungrily on the pulsing end of the sonic.

The Doctor reached out to Mae and helped her back to her feet, taking her hand to stop her from falling again. 'Run!' he hissed.

They ran, their feet alternately slipping on the ice or sinking into the snow. The trouble was that, with the rain in their eyes, they couldn't tell which was which and that was slowing them down.

After a few moments, they paused to catch their breath. 'Who are those people?' asked Mae.

'I don't know,' the Doctor admitted. 'But they don't seem very happy to see us.'

Then he heard the crunch of footsteps in the snow behind him and he spun round to see the other members of the gang approaching. They were surrounded.

The Doctor pulled his sonic out of his pocket again and whipped it back and forth. 'Stay back,' he warned. 'I'm not afraid to use this!' He made to press the button on the handle, then realised there wasn't a button there at all. He sighed. He hadn't taken out his sonic screwdriver after all. It was a carrot.

'Look,' he said. 'You've got all this snow, and I've got a carrot. If it turns out that Mae has three pieces of coal and a top hat in her pocket, maybe we can come to some sort of arrangement...'

He tossed the carrot to the ground where the three nearest of their attackers dropped to their knees to scrabble about for it. The Doctor finally located his sonic screwdriver and held it at arm's length, its green light illuminating the pale faces of the approaching assailants.

'Stay back!' he warned, swinging the sonic from figure to figure. But they continued to shuffle forward, their eyes fixed on the bright emerald glow at its tip.

'They don't want to hurt you!' cried a voice.

The Doctor turned. There was a figure standing on top of one of the houses, silhouetted against the gleaming white sky. 'What do they want?' he shouted back.

'Your possessions,' the figure bellowed. It was a deep voice. A man's. 'Give them something of yours and they'll leave you alone – for a short while at least.'

Keeping the sonic chirping at arm's length, the Doctor released Mae's waist and began to root through his jacket pockets with his free hand. Mae pulled the satsuma the Doctor had given her earlier from her skirt pocket. 'Does he mean like this?'

The Doctor shrugged. 'Got to be worth a try…'

Mae hurled the piece of fruit over the heads of two of their attackers. Both of them – a man and a woman, dived after it and began to fight over it in the snow.

'Keep going,' cried the man from the top of the house.

The Doctor pulled his hand from his pocket and looked down at it. He was clutching a silver fountain pen.

'What are you waiting for?' cried Mae. 'Throw it!'

'But this is an original Paul E. Wirt pen!' exclaimed the Doctor. 'Mark Twain gave it to me after he'd written the first draft of *Huckleberry Finn* with it. Terrible speller, I had to do a lot of editing before he could submit the manuscript.'

'Then choose something else!' bellowed Mae.

Stuffing the pen back into his pocket, the Doctor

produced a large key, then a computer mouse, and finally a baseball. The group around them had begun to realise that the sonic wasn't doing them any harm and they were creeping ever closer. 'Throw it!' yelled Mae. 'Now!'

'It's signed by Babe Ruth,' hissed the Doctor, turning it to display the autograph.

'I don't care!' Mae snatched the baseball from his hand and pitched it hard onto the ground in front of them. Every single one of the attackers fell upon it, grunting and lashing out in an effort to obtain it.

'This way,' cried the man. 'Now!' He leapt down from the roof of the house, landing nimbly in the soft snow beneath. Then he opened the door to one of the few remaining houses with its windows intact.

The Doctor grabbed Mae's hand and they ran, dashing past the figure and inside the dwelling.

It was roomier inside than the Doctor had expected, and appeared to be built into the side of the hill behind it. But he didn't have time to waste in exploring. The man from the rooftop had now opened a metal trapdoor in the centre of the floor and was gesturing for them all to climb down the narrow steps and into the darkness beyond.

Ushering Mae ahead of him, the Doctor did as he was told and was closely followed by their new-found friend. There wasn't much room at the bottom of the ladder, and both Mae and the Doctor found themselves pressed up against another figure.

'Hello,' said the Doctor, holding out a wet hand in the dim light from the room above. But that was quickly cut off as the trapdoor closed with a clunk.

'Ssshhh!' instructed the man who had led them into the house. They fell silent, just as the window shattered in the room above. The Doctor could hear footsteps climb in, crunching onto the pieces of broken glass. First just one of their attackers, then a second and eventually too many to distinguish individually.

They lumbered around above them for a few minutes then, with a grunt of frustration, they began to leave the way they had arrived.

'Well,' said the Doctor after a few moments of quiet. 'This is cosy, isn't it?' He lit the end of the sonic, bathing them in green light. He still couldn't see his rescuers properly, but it gave him the opportunity to look around the space they were in. There was a door behind the second man.

'It's just the entrance to the lower floor,' said the man from the roof. 'I didn't want to take you any further while the Wanters were up there in case they heard the door creak. These old places aren't exactly well maintained.'

'Wanters?' asked Mae. 'What are they?'

'You've never heard of Wanters before?' said the second figure. 'Where are you from?'

'Long story,' said the Doctor. 'But now that we're not in danger of being heard, why don't we go a little further in and make ourselves comfortable?'

The second figure turned and pushed the inner door. As predicted, it creaked loudly as it swung open. By the light of the sonic, the Doctor and Mae could just about make out a long corridor stretching away into the darkness.

'Hold on,' said one of the men. 'There should be an oil lamp here somewhere.' He struck a match and a light flared into life. The Doctor blinked at the sudden absence of blackness then, when his eyes had adjusted, he turned to thank the two men who had saved Mae and himself.

He stopped, a wide grin splitting his features. 'Oh, that is just brilliant! Isn't it, Mae?'

Mae stared at the men. Both of them were dressed in baggy, multicoloured suits, both had white faces and red noses, and both wore shaggy, rainbow wigs. 'You're clowns!' she gasped.

'Well, of course,' said the red-nosed figure from the roof. 'That's Flip Flop, and I'm Wobblebottom. You were expecting someone other than clowns?'

'Actually no,' said the Doctor gleefully. He took Wobblebottom's hand and pumped it. 'A journey to a distant ice world in a stolen ambulance and a gang of thieves who fight over a baseball and a satsuma. Why wouldn't there be clowns waiting to rescue us?'

He turned to get a better look along the corridor. Doors led off from both sides and he tried the first to find a well-appointed bedroom behind it. 'This is fantastic!' he beamed. 'I expect you come down here to get away from the cold weather.'

'No,' said Flip Flop matter-of-factly. 'We come down here to get away from the bear attacks.'

'Turn around now!' yelled Clara. 'We have to go back for them!' They had left the Doctor and Mae just a few minutes earlier, but had already lost sight of them in the rainstorm. The windscreen wipers thumped back and forth across the glass, but did very little to help visibility.

'I'm trying to!' shouted Warren. 'But there are snowdrifts on either side of us. If I turn here, we'll just get stuck again, and where will that leave us?'

Clara reached for her door handle.

'What are you doing?' cried Warren, grabbing her arm and pulling it away from the door.

'Going to help the Doctor!'

'Don't be stupid! This isn't a road – we're just driving over snow and ice. Even if you could find your way back, you'd only run straight into those lunatics who attacked us.'

'Well, we have to do something.'

'We're going to,' Warren assured her. He reached inside his jacket and pulled his gun from its holster. 'Take that.'

Clara took the gun awkwardly, and wrapped her hand around the polished wooden grip on the handle. She kept her finger away from the trigger.

Warren nodded and began to drive once more.

Steering the ambulance was proving tricky. The ice-cold rain was freezing on top of the snow already lying on the ground, and the vehicle was drifting from side to side occasionally catching one of the mounds of snow beside them and releasing a torrent of white powder.

'It's getting wider,' said Warren, pulling the wheel gently to the right to correct a slight skid. 'If it keeps up like this, we'll be able to turn back in a few minutes.'

'Stop!' cried Clara suddenly.

Warren hit the brakes, but the ambulance slid on a few yards, gently bumping to a stop against one of the path's snowy walls.

'What is it?' he asked.

'Out there,' said Clara, pointing through the windscreen. 'There's something in front of us.'

Warren wiped the condensation from the inside of the window and tried to see what Clara was looking at. A gust of wind cleared the rain to one side for a split second and he saw it. 'A mound of snow,' he said. 'Well spotted. If we'd run into that we wouldn't be going anywhere. I'll clear it.'

He grabbed the piece of wood that had once decorated the inside of the door and began to climb out.

'Be careful,' said Clara.

Warren nodded, and stepped back out into the

cold. Clara watched as he approached the pile of snow, his figure lit up in the ambulance's headlights. Then without warning – the snow began to move. It rose up into the air and turned to face the FBI agent.

It wasn't a mound of snow. It was a pure white bear.

Warren stared up at the creature in horror. Now standing on its hind legs, the bear was at least twelve feet in height, and it had razor-sharp tusks protruding from the corners of its mouth – a sabre-toothed polar bear.

The animal roared, the sound reverberating deep in Warren's stomach. He wanted to run. To turn and jump back into the ambulance and drive away as fast as he could. But he couldn't move. He was rooted to the spot with fear. This was where it would all end. On some alien planet where no one would ever find his body – if there was much left of it to find after this massive bear had finished with him, that was.

The bear lumbered towards Warren, and he suddenly found his feet. He walked backwards, keeping his eyes on the bear holding up the piece of panelling from the ambulance door as though it could protect him from the animal's teeth and claws – but it was all he had.

One swipe of the bear's massive paw split the wood in two, sending Warren stumbling, his feet sliding on the ice. He glanced quickly to his left and right – looking for an escape route. But all he could see was more snow. If he tried to run. The creature would be on him in seconds.

He felt the back of his legs bump against something hard. The front bumper of the ambulance. He reached back to feel around on the vehicle's bonnet with his fingertips, trying to work out which door he was closest to. The engine was still running, and the metal felt warm beneath his fingers. Warren wondered briefly whether the sensation was the last feeling he would ever have.

Just a few feet away now, the bear continued to lumber towards him, still raised up on its back legs. It roared once more and lashed out with its paw, sharp talons cutting through the material of Warren's jacket, and then—

Bang!

The bear started as a gunshot rang out, but it didn't take long to regain its nerve. It roared angrily and continued to lurch forward.

Bang!

This time the bear paused. Warren finally found the power to move and spun round to find Clara standing in the rain behind him, gun aimed at the animal.

'Get back in the ambulance,' he ordered, running for the driver's door. Another roar echoed out from the hills of snow over to his right. Then another – from the left. The bear had friends, and the gunshots had attracted their attention.

Clara and Warren leapt back into the ambulance and slammed the doors. Warren revved the engine, driving forward straight at the angry bear. He caught it on its left leg, sending it spinning and losing the remaining wing mirror in the process. The burst of speed put the ambulance into a spin and he fought with the wheel, trying to keep the vehicle from smashing into one of the snow banks.

To Clara's amazement, the ambulance spun exactly 180 degrees, and they found that they were now facing back in the direction of the Doctor and Mae. She and Warren allowed themselves a brief smile, and then they were off, swerving around the now unmoving figure of the bear they had hit, and gaining speed. They were on their way back to help.

And then a huge paw tipped with long, off-white claws exploded through the window beside her.

Chapter 11

'You're from another planet?' Wobblebottom paused in the midst of lighting the fire in the grate and turned to look at the Doctor, who was pacing up and down, his feet squelching with every step.

They were in a sparse, yet agreeable living room which lay behind a door further along the underground tunnel. As with the bedroom they had seen, the walls, ceiling and floor were all made of metal. Four armchairs sat in a semicircle facing the fire, their material was well worn but, as Mae sank into one at the invitation of the clowns, she discovered they were very comfortable.

'We're from two other planets, if you want to be technical about it,' said the Doctor. 'But Earth will do for now. What planet is this?'

'You don't know?' asked Flip Flop.

'Not a clue,' beamed the Doctor. 'That's half the fun of it.'

'This is Semtis,' said Wobblebottom, turning his attention back to the fire. He made sure the wood was burning properly, then stepped aside to allow the Doctor and Mae to get closer to the flames.

'Semtis!' exclaimed the Doctor, holding his soggy trouser legs in front of the fire. 'Gosh! If I remember correctly – and it's very rare that I don't remember everything correctly – that's in the top left-hand corner of the Andromeda galaxy, from the point of view of Earth, that is. You *are* a long way from home, Mae.'

'We're in another galaxy?' said Mae, holding her palms out towards the warming flames.

The Doctor nodded. 'Two and a half million light years from your own. Or less if you wait a bit, they're due to collide in about...' He checked his watch. 'Four billion years' time.'

Mae blinked, clearly not convinced. 'And the people here just happen to be humans, who speak English?'

'Humans are pretty much universal,' the Doctor pointed out. 'And it'll be the TARDIS that's translating for us. It may be over two and a half million light years away but, if you go via the wormhole, it's just a couple of miles. Easily within translation range.'

'Wormhole?' asked Wobblebottom.

The Doctor nodded. 'Connecting Semtis and Earth. It's how we got here.' He stripped off his jacket and lay it in front of the fire to dry it out. 'Just what I needed – another soggy bow tie moment. Seems to be happening a lot lately.'

Mae leaned forward, holding her palms towards the roaring fire. 'I prefer it down here to out there.'

'It's lovely,' said the Doctor to the clowns. 'But we can't stay for long. We have to find our friends, and I want to talk to someone here about the Shroud.'

Flip Flop winced at the name. 'The Shroud destroyed our world,' he said. 'Turned us into a society of tribes – like the Wanters you encountered outside.'

'You called them that before,' said Mae. 'What are "Wanters"?'

Wobblebottom sat forward on his chair, his face grim, despite the painted-on smile. 'It was around the end of the last season that we started seeing faces,' he explained. 'Just in patterns on our walls, or in cracks on the ice clinging to the window panes. All people who had died. People we missed. And then the women in blue appeared.'

Mae and the Doctor shared a glance. This sounded very familiar.

'They held our hands, and drained our minds,' Wobblebottom continued. 'We tried to rid ourselves of the Shroud, but every time we tried to save someone, they died.' He stared into the crackling flames of the fire for a moment. 'They ate our grief.'

'That's what's happening right now on Earth,' said the Doctor. 'I have to find a way to stop them.'

'You can't,' said Flip Flop. 'The Shroud are unstoppable. We tried everything.'

'But why did those people – the Wanters – act the way they did when they saw us?' asked Mae.

'It's down to the human brain,' said the Doctor. 'When one emotion – such as grief – is completely eradicated from a person's mind, another emotion grows to fill the gap, giving it dominance over any other feelings that person may have and utterly controlling them. With these Wanters, it appears that jealousy took over.'

'That's right,' said Wobblebottom. 'They want anything they don't have – although when they get it, they don't know what to do with it. They simply cast their new belongings aside and hunt for more.'

'And I'm guessing they're not the only "tribe", as you put it,' said the Doctor.

'The Ragers are the worst,' said Flip Flop. 'Completely controlled by anger, they do nothing but attack and destroy. The Tremblers are terrified of them.'

'People overrun with fear?' said Mae.

Wobblebottom nodded. 'They don't give us any trouble. They stay cowering in their homes for the most part, but we still try to find a way to look after them. They can feed themselves, but that's about all.'

'We?' said the Doctor. 'How many of you are there?'

'Almost five hundred now,' said Flip Flop. 'Unaffected people are gradually arriving from all over Semtis, looking for somewhere safe to live. We train them up as clowns so they can help us in our work.

'What is your work, exactly?' asked Mae.

'We help people,' said Wobblebottom. 'It took us a while to work out how, but we've discovered that we can restore the emotions that Wanters and Tremblers are missing. It even works with some Ragers.'

'So they go back to normal?'

'As near as we can get them to it,' Wobblebottom replied. 'Anyone who's been restored needs regular therapy sessions to keep their emotions in balance, but so far we've had very few failures. Many of our patients have now become well enough to join the Clowns and look after new arrivals.'

'Ah, the human race!' cried the Doctor. 'It doesn't matter which planet you evolved on, you all want the same thing – to help your fellow man. Splendid stuff!'

'No, it isn't,' said Mae. 'It isn't splendid at all. Is this what's going to happen on Earth after the Shroud have finished with us and moved on? We'll just be planet of Ragers and Wanters?'

'Not if I've got anything to do with it,' said the

Doctor, snatching up his partially dry coat and slipping it back on. 'I'd like to see one of these restorations in action.'

'Not a problem,' said Wobblebottom. 'Just come back to our camp with us.'

'Although we can't go back empty-handed,' Flip Flop pointed out.

'He's right,' said Wobblebottom. 'We've been following that gang of Wanters since first light, planning to bring one back to base with us.'

Mae gasped. 'You mean you kidnap them?'

'They don't exactly volunteer for restoration,' Wobblebottom pointed out. 'And it's gradually making the world safer for other people.'

'Very true,' said the Doctor. 'So let's go out and catch us a Wanter!'

Clara opened her eyes, but her vision remained blurred. Not that there was much to see. She was lying in the snow, and was very, very cold. Behind her, the ambulance – what was left of it – lay on its side, wheels spinning and the top half of a sabre-toothed polar bear sticking out from beneath. Thankfully, the bear was very dead.

I'm going to be just as dead myself if I can't find shelter, she thought. Warren, too.

That was a point. Where was Warren? You'd think his loud suit would be easy to spot against the harsh whiteness of the snow.

Clara heard a groan, and dragged herself in its direction. She found Warren half-buried in a snowdrift, unmoving. She began to crawl over to him. She vaguely remembered the accident – Warren spinning the steering wheel as the bear attacked, then skidding into a wall of snow and the ambulance flipping over on top of the creature. The crash had scared the other bear away, but it would be back before long – especially if there was fresh meat on offer.

She reached Warren and collapsed in the snow beside him. Her head was pounding. Had she hit it on something when the ambulance turned over? She couldn't remember. All she could hear was the thump, thump, thump of the pain behind her eyes – and something else... A squeaking sound. *Squeak, squeak, squeak, squeak.*

Clara's vision began to fade again, just as a huge pair of shoes came into view. They were making the squeaking noise! *Squeak, squeak, squeak, squeak.* The owner of the giant shoes stood over her, his curly hair ruffling in the breeze.

'Oh, no you don't!'

There was a hiss of gas, then everything went black.

'I haven't played this for years!' cried the Doctor, tooting out a rendition of 'Three Blind Mice' on his recorder. 'I didn't even realise I had it in my pocket!'

Mae crouched behind the splintered wood of the broken door with the two Clowns. 'Are you sure the Wanters will come for it?' she hissed.

'Of course,' said the Doctor. 'I mean, who wouldn't want a great recorder like this?' His brow furrowed as an unpleasant thought occurred. 'I don't have to give it away, do I?'

'No,' said Wobblebottom. 'Just get one of the Wanters close enough, and we'll do the rest.'

And so the Doctor began to pace up and down outside the row of abandoned houses, playing tunes on his recorder.

'Do you have to skip as well?' asked Mae with a smile.

'I'm not skipping,' said the Doctor, pausing halfway through a jazz version of 'Yankee Doodle Dandy'. 'I'm marching. Like in a marching band.' He went back to playing, taking care to tone down his footwork.

'There!' said Flip Flop, pointing to a large snowdrift. 'I saw movement.'

'I see him, too,' said Wobblebottom. 'OK, Doctor, you've got company. Keep playing, but don't make eye contact. Let him come to you.'

The Doctor switched from 'Yankee Doodle Dandy' to 'When The Saints Go Marching In'.

The Wanter moved incredibly fast. One moment he was watching the Doctor warily from his hiding place and, the next, he had hold of the end of the recorder and was trying to pull it from his grasp.

'Now!' yelled Flip Flop.

Mae watched in amazement as the Clowns leapt out on either side of the Wanter. Before the man could react, gas poured from the oversized plastic flowers attached to the lapels of their jackets.

'Hold your breath!' ordered Wobblebottom. The Doctor stopped playing, his last note echoing off the walls inside the abandoned house.

The gas worked instantly, knocking the Wanter out cold. He slumped to the ground.

'OK,' said Wobblebottom. 'The rest of the gas has blown away. We can all breathe again.'

The Doctor continued playing from where he'd left off.

'He said breathe, not play,' Flip Flop pointed out.

The Doctor reluctantly lowered the recorder. 'I was enjoying that,' he muttered. He slipped the instrument back into his coat. 'Now what?'

Flip Flop and Wobblebottom grabbed the unconscious Wanter underneath his arms and hauled him to his feet. 'We get this guy back to our camp before the others in his gang come looking for him.'

They led the Doctor and Mae back down into the underground tunnels, where Flip Flop retrieved a metal cart from one of the bedrooms. They carefully laid the Wanter down in it. Then, an oil lamp in his hand to light the way, Wobblebottom took them deeper into the passageways.

They had been walking for around twenty minutes when Mae spoke up. 'Why us?' she asked. 'Why are there people like us who have escaped being devoured?'

'I've got a theory,' said Wobblebottom. 'With me, I think it's because I was in the security forces, out on the street, helping people and – occasionally – dealing with criminals and accidents. I saw some terrible things, and frequently had to pass on bad news to loved ones.'

'Just like Warren,' said the Doctor. 'One of our friends,' he added for the benefit of the Clowns. 'He was like you – a law enforcement agent. Probably saw more than his fair share of grief. And you, Mae. All those stories in the newspaper. All that misery. It toughened you up. Gave you the strength to fight off the advances of the Shroud.'

The tunnel began to widen, and the Doctor could see lights ahead. Voices echoed off the metal walls of the tunnel and, after a moment, the group stepped into a vast underground cavern.

'Welcome to Clown Camp!' grinned Wobblebottom.

The Doctor and Mae stood near the entrance, drinking in the sight before them. The room looked as though it had once been some kind of theatre or performance venue, but the seats had been removed to make room for scores of small, multicoloured tents and tepees. Spotlights shone down from a ceiling high above, hidden among long lengths of cloth stretched out to resemble the roof of a circus big top.

Up on a stage, a group of young Clowns juggled, danced, spun plates, tumbled and chased each other with fake custard pies. And everywhere there was music. Bright, jolly, happy music. More motley-painted people played on instruments from wherever they sat or stood. It was all the Doctor could do not to whip out his recorder and join in. Instead he stood and smiled his widest smile.

'Oh, this is amazing!'

A man dressed in an acrobat's costume hurried their way, carrying a tray of drinks. 'Welcome!' he beamed. 'I'm Jorge. Please, help yourself!'

Mae accepted a glass from the tray. 'Thank you, Jorge,' she said.

Flip Flop smiled. 'Up until two weeks ago, Jorge was a Wanter, just like this guy. We restored him in less than eight sessions. Let's hope it's as easy this time.' He turned and pushed the cart containing the sleeping Wanter towards an archway on the far side of the hall.

'Is that where you keep them?' asked the Doctor. 'The Ragers, Wanters and Tremblers?'

'In separate rooms,' said Wobblebottom. 'Would you like to see?'

He led the Doctor and Mae through the arch

and into a corridor that looked almost identical to the one beneath the row of ruined houses – except this one was brightly lit and filled with the music that played in the main hall, pumped through by speakers fastened to the walls.

Each of the doors along the corridor had a barred window cut into it, and the Doctor stopped at the first one to peer through. Inside the room, two women and a man sat in armchairs, expressions of terror etched onto their faces. One of the women saw the Doctor looking at her and she squealed, drawing her knees up to her chest and pulling herself into a ball.

'It's OK,' the Doctor said. 'You're in a good place, here. These people are going to help you to smile again.' He turned to find Mae standing beside him, also looking into the room.

'This is awful,' she said.

Wobblebottom rested a hand on her shoulder. 'Only for now,' he assured her. 'You saw Jorge – the acrobat who offered you drinks. These people will be just like him very soon.'

The next room contained only the sleeping Wanter they had brought with them. Flip Flop was carefully putting the man in the recovery position on a fold-out bed.

'We have a dozen rooms for our patients,' said Wobblebottom as he led the Doctor and Mae past more groups of Tremblers and Wanters, the latter pushing their arms out through the barred windows to try and grab the visitors' clothing as they passed. 'But this is where it gets a little distressing…'

They reached a bolted door at the end of the corridor, which was guarded by a Clown wearing a curly, yellow wig and large shoes. Wobblebottom nodded, and the guard slid back the metal latches and pulled it open. Instantly, the Doctor and Mae became aware of angry shouts and screams. There were three more doors beyond this one. The Doctor stepped up to the barred window cut into the first.

The room was empty of all furniture, which Wobblebottom explained was so the Ragers couldn't use it to hurt themselves. The man inside was in his 40s, slightly overweight and short. At the sight of the visitors, he roared furiously and ran at the door, throwing himself at it with such force that Mae jumped involuntarily.

'It's all right,' said the Doctor. 'I'm a friend.' But the words did nothing to change the man's behaviour. He began to rain blows down on the door, tearing the skin from his already bloodied knuckles.

'I knew him,' said Wobblebottom sadly. 'In real life, before the Shroud, I mean. He lived on my street. Ran a market stall selling vegetables. You couldn't meet a nicer, more gentle person.' As if to disprove the description, the man ran head first at the door, smashing his forehead against the metal and causing himself to stumble back. The Doctor quickly moved to the next room.

Mae followed, glancing in at the man as she passed. She couldn't help but feel sorry for him, with his cheeks flushed purple with the rage he felt, but could never understand. And his eyes... She couldn't look at them for long. The man's eyes were bulging out of his head, as though they were about to burst. She hurried to join the Doctor and Wobblebottom as they approached the next room.

'The ones that batter the door are bad enough,' said Wobblebottom. 'But it's the quiet ones you want to watch out for. They can turn on you without warning.'

The Doctor stepped up to the door and looked inside – then he gripped the bars of the small window so tightly that his knuckles whitened. 'Open this door at once!' he demanded.

'I can't,' said Wobblebottom. 'It could be dangerous...'

'Do it!'

Wobblebottom called down the corridor to the guard. 'Dolfini...'

The Clown's large shoes squeaked as he ran down to join them, unclipping a large bundle of keys from his belt. Finding the right one, Dolfini unlocked the door and the Doctor rushed inside. Following him, Mae gasped at what she saw.

Lying on the floor in the corner of the room was Clara.

Chapter 12

The Doctor followed the directions Wobblebottom had given him and carried Clara into a tepee near the rear of the auditorium. Warren was already inside, a female Clown in a fluorescent nurse's outfit dabbing at a nasty-looking cut on his cheek.

'Doctor!' he exclaimed. 'Is she OK?'

The Doctor laid Clara down on a pile of blankets. 'A little concussed, but she'll live,' he said, accepting a damp cloth from the nurse and using it to mop her brow. Mae hurried over to Warren and hugged him tightly.

Dolfini appeared in the entrance to the tent. 'I'm really sorry,' he said, wringing his white-gloved hands together. 'I found them both in the snow beside the wreck of some weird vehicle. The man was unconscious, and the girl was crawling over to him. I thought she was a Rager who'd attacked him, so I used my knockout gas on her.'

'It's OK,' said the Doctor. 'I know it was an honest mistake.'

Dolfini nodded and stomped away, his shoes squeaking.

'What happened to you both?' Mae asked.

Warren told the Doctor and Mae about their encounter with the bears and about the accident they'd had while trying to escape, although he couldn't remember much after that. 'The next thing I know, I'm lying here with Orma looking after me.' He smiled at the Clown nurse, who blushed beneath her white make-up.

'Orma!' cried Mae. 'That was the name you used in the wormhole.'

Warren nodded. 'She lost contact with her brother when the Shroud attacked. I think that may have been whose memories I encountered.'

'Doctor, you and your friends might want to come and see this...' Wobblebottom had poked his head through the tent flap and was beckoning for the group to join him.

The Doctor glanced down at Clara. 'It's OK,' said Orma with a smile. 'She'll be fine with me.'

The Doctor led Mae and Warren out of the tent. Wobblebottom gestured to the stage at the front of the room. The performers had moved to the sides, allowing a pair of larger Clowns to lead a man onto the centre of the stage. It was the Wanter they had captured earlier, now fully awake. He reached out towards the props, but the large Clowns held him firmly in place.

Wobblebottom turned to Mae, sensing her distress. 'We have to hold him still,' he explained, 'at least at first. For the restoration sessions to work, the patient must remain in one place, from where he can hear and see everything that happens around him.' He took a whistle from his pocket, raised it to his lips and blew it. 'Let the treatment begin!' he cried.

The musicians around the room began to play a new song – rousing, upbeat and jolly. At the sound, the Clowns on stage began to perform together. They spun around the Wanter, laughing and smiling. Some of them juggled lengths of brightly coloured cloth between them, while others rode on unicycles or twisted balloons into animals. The overall effect was a dizzying spectacle of colour and sound.

The Wanter turned his head from side to side, not knowing which way to look. He thrust out his hand more than once, reaching to try and grab a juggling club or balloon animal. Occasionally, such an item was handed to him by a laughing performer, who quickly grabbed a new prop from the side of the stage and joined in with the fun once more. Everything the Wanter was given, he immediately dropped to the floor as he focused on the spectacle around him.

Then, after almost ten minutes, the Wanter laughed. It was a small laugh – barely a chuckle – and could easily have been missed among the choreographed chaos but the Clowns let out a rousing cheer as soon as they saw it. Wobblebottom blew his whistle again, the performance ended, and the man was led off stage.

'He'll be taken back to his room for food and rest now,' said Wobblebottom. 'We'll run another therapy session with him tomorrow and, if all goes well, he could be joining the Clowns around us in just over a week.'

The Doctor spun to face Wobblebottom, his eyes sparkling with sheer joy. 'I've seen a lot of wonderful things in my time,' he said. 'Kind gestures, selfless acts, caring behaviour… But that is one of the best.' With that he grabbed the Clown by his cheeks and planted a friendly kiss on his forehead.

'They're weren't so wonderful with me,' groaned a voice behind them.

The Doctor, Warren and Mae turned to find Clara heading their way.

'There you are!' cried the Doctor, sweeping her into his arms. 'You're up and about, then?'

'You try sleeping with that racket going on,' Clara whined.

'Careful,' warned Mae teasingly. 'Don't moan too much or they might mistake you for a Rager again.'

Clara accepted a drink from a passing Clown's tray and downed it in one. 'So,' she said. 'What did I miss?'

'Wobblebottom here has been showing us how the Clowns restore the victims of the Shroud,' said the Doctor. 'And it's got me thinking... What would happen if we were to try the same with people who were still attached to the Shroud? People who hadn't yet had all their grief consumed.'

'I've no idea,' admitted the Clown. 'We didn't come up with the process until after the Shroud had finished with us and moved on. Aside from the few of us who were spared, everyone on Semtis falls into one of the tribal groups you've already seen – as far as we know at least.'

'I wasn't talking about Semtis,' said the Doctor. 'I wish I'd known about the Shroud and been here to help you at the time, but it's too late for that, I'm afraid. I'm talking about Earth.'

'You think we could free people from the Shroud by performing for them?' asked Warren. 'You think it could sever the links?'

'I don't know,' said the Doctor. 'But I'm willing to try.' He checked his watch. 'We have less than five hours until the entire planet is infected and people reach an acceptance of their fate. By then, it will be too late.'

'But so many people are already being feasted on, Doctor,' said Mae. 'How can we round up enough performers in five hours?'

'We may not have to,' replied the Doctor, turning to Wobblebottom. 'Will you help us?'

The Clown's painted eyes grew wide. 'You want us to come with you to another planet?'

'Just for a little while,' said the Doctor. 'It's only a short hop through the wormhole and, if we succeed in banishing the Shroud, I'll bring you all back first class in my TARDIS.'

'You keep talking about a wormhole,' said Wobblebottom. 'What do you mean?'

'I've got this one,' said Warren. 'It's like a tunnel through time and space – a bit like a sock with the foot cut off. It bends the rules of the universe to connect two locations together, allowing you to pass from one to the other while avoiding a trip that could take thousands of years.'

'Very well put,' beamed the Doctor. 'The Shroud used a wormhole to travel from Semtis to Earth,' he continued. 'It's a bit of a bumpy journey, with a few living nightmares along the way – but all in all a fun ride.' He turned to Wobblebottom. 'Will you help us?'

'Well, who's going to turn down the chance to do that?' beamed the Clown. 'I can't spare everyone – there's still important work to be done here – but I reckon I can round up a troupe of about a hundred or so performers.'

'You're still forgetting something important,' said

Clara. 'We lost the ambulance in a battle with a bear or three. We need a vehicle to get back through it, or we'll be blasted into atoms as soon as we pass through the portal.'

'She's right,' said Warren. 'And it will need to be something big if there are going to be over a hundred of us on the return journey.'

'We can handle that as well,' said Wobblebottom. He produced his whistle again and blew it. 'Bring out the wheels!'

After a moment, a new sound could be heard over the constant music.

Putta-putta-choof! Putta-putta-choof! Putta-putta-choof!

And a tiny car painted in orange and green flowers chugged into view.

'Wait…' said Clara with a frown. 'We're all going back to Earth in that thing?'

'Of course!' exclaimed the Doctor, grinning from ear to ear. 'Inspired by Gallifreyan technology such as the Type 40 TARDIS, you're looking at just about the only other dimensionally transcendental vehicle in the universe. The clown car!'

Mae climbed into the back of the clown car and chuckled to herself. The Doctor was right. It really was bigger on the inside. She'd visited the circus with her grandmother as a girl, and had always wondered how so many clowns had managed to fit inside such a tiny vehicle. Could those comedy cars have worked the same way?

A face painted in bright colours appeared through the doorway and handed her a box which she knew would be packed with props. Juggling balls, hooters, magic tricks and more – all of which they would use to try to free the people of Earth from the terrible clutches of the Shroud. It was going to be an uphill battle, but the Doctor assured her that he still had a trick or two up his sleeve that would help.

Mae tucked the box carefully to one side, then accepted a bundle of costume bags from another Clown. Back in high school, she and her drama group had toured a play they'd written around elementary schools in the area. Getting the clown car ready for the journey home felt very similar to packing up their small van for the tour.

Two Clowns later, Clara appeared in the doorway. 'How are you getting on?'

'Still plenty of room,' said Clara, gesturing to the empty space inside the car. 'It shouldn't be a problem getting us all inside.'

'That's good,' said Clara, 'because the Doctor wants to—' she stopped, staring past Mae and out through the window behind her.

'What's wrong?' Mae asked. But Clara had disappeared. Mae climbed out of the car and hurried after her. She found Clara crouched before a young girl of around 4 or 5 years old, holding a picture book.

'It's her,' said Clara, looking up at Mae. 'The girl I saw in my dream in the wormhole.' She turned back to the girl. 'What's your name?'

'Jaz,' said the girl. She glanced at Clara's hands, shaking slightly as they gripped her shoulders. 'Are you a Trembler?'

'No,' smiled Clara. 'I haven't been affected by the Shroud.'

'You're lucky,' said Jaz. 'My mother was. She's a Trembler now, but Wobblebottom says he can restore her. I hope he can, because she has the prettiest smile.'

Clara pulled the girl into her and held her tightly. 'If Wobblebottom says he can do it, then I believe him.'

Jaz beamed at the thought. 'I have to go now,' she said. 'I'm not allowed in my mother's room until she's been treated, but I sit outside every day and read her a story.'

'That's a wonderful thing to do,' said Clara, ruffling the girl's hair. 'Your mother must be so proud to have a daughter like you.' She watched as Jaz raced away towards the entrance to the cells. 'I always thought a world without grief would be a good thing,' she said, standing up. 'But it's not.'

'No, it's not,' said the Doctor, approaching with Warren. 'Humans are incredibly complicated beings, and everything inside their heads is there for a reason. Take just one part away and the whole thing goes out of whack.'

'Maybe we'd be better off without any emotions at all,' Warren suggested.

'You wouldn't say that if you'd met some of the emotionless monsters I've had to face,' he said. 'What's happening on Semtis may not be perfect – but it works. Human beings doing what they can for their fellow man. Now – I think we're just about loaded. Let's go and stop this from ever happening on Earth.'

One by one, the Clowns chosen for the journey climbed into the back of the clown car and found an empty seat. Mae found herself sitting between Orma the nurse and a man dressed as a hobo clown in ragged clothes.

Warren and Clara buckled themselves in along the opposite wall. 'Let's hope this trip is a little less traumatic,' Clara said.

The Doctor climbed into the front seat with Flip Flop and Wobblebottom. 'Ready?' he smiled.

Wobblebottom nodded. 'Time to set a big foot on another world!'

Flip Flop started the engine and drove the tiny car to a ramp at the back of the room. A clown in oily overalls winched a handle and a door cranked open, allowing them to motor out into the ice and snow.

Putta-putta-choof! Putta-putta-choof! Putta-putta-choof!

The car skidded slightly on the slippery ground,

and the Doctor wound down his window to peer out. 'Are you sure we can make it back to where you found us?' he asked, studying the slippery surface beneath them.

'No problem,' beamed Flip Flop. He flicked a switch on the car's dashboard and rows of sharp metal spikes sprang out from the tyres, digging into the ice for grip.

The Doctor beamed happily as he wound his window back up. 'Love a Clown!'

The journey back to the wormhole was incident – and bear – free. Flip Flop pulled up before the shimmering portal, allowing the Doctor to jump out and wave his sonic screwdriver over its surface.

'Got to reset the polarity,' he called over the chirrup of the gadget. Satisfied the task was done, he jumped back into the car. 'Can I have your attention,' he called to the group sitting in the back. 'Please ensure your safety belts are fastened and your tray tables are in the upright position. In the event of turbulence or experiencing flashes of someone else's terrifying memories, please try to remain calm. Should the oxygen fail, you will all turn blue and choke within a matter of seconds, so let's cross our fingers and hope that doesn't happen.

'Exits will be available when the doors fall off comically, or via the ejector seat – which I've just realised I'm sitting in. We do hope you will choose Wormhole Travel for your next nightmare-fuelled journey to a distant world. Now, sit back, relax, and enjoy the journey.'

He turned to Flip Flop, lowering his voice. 'Put your foot down and don't stop until we come out the other side, no matter what happens.'

With a nod, Flip Flop put the clown car in gear and drove into the wormhole.

Chapter 13

The clown car burst out of the shimmering portal in the hospital wall, the spikes in its tyres digging up the tarmac of the car park. Flip Flop hit the brakes, bringing the vehicle to a juddering halt.

'Wobblebottom!' cried the Doctor, scanning him with his sonic. The Clown's pale make-up glowed green.

'What's wrong with him?' asked Flip Flop.

'He's caught up in someone's memories,' explained the Doctor. 'It happened to us on the way to Semtis. He should be OK in a few minutes.'

As if on cue, Wobblebottom's eyes flickered open and he groaned. 'He was trapped,' he said. 'A boy – a teenager. Trapped in the underground rooms of his house. His parents were Ragers, tearing the ground floor apart. He… was signalling for help with a radio. I remember the frequency.'

'Then I know you'll be able to find him when you get back home,' said the Doctor. He turned to Clara, Warren and Mae in the back of the car. 'How is everyone?'

'A couple of them had memory flashes,' Clara replied. 'But they're all coming round now.'

'Good,' said the Doctor. 'Everyone out.'

Steadily, the clowns began to climb out of the tiny vehicle, one after another. They emerged into the late-afternoon sunshine, gazing around in wonder at what to them was a bizarre new world. Two of them nervously approached a tree and ran their hands over the bark, giggling.

'What is this place?' asked Orma, looking up at the building.

'A hospital,' said Warren. 'With doctors and nurses. They treat people who are sick.'

Orma glanced down at her own fluorescent pink nurse's uniform. 'I guess I'd fit right in then,' she smiled.

Warren smiled. 'They wouldn't notice a thing.'

'Doctor,' said Mae. 'Look!'

The Doctor turned to find dozens of people walking down the steps from the hospital entrance, each one holding hands with a blue-veiled woman.

'Over there, too,' said Clara, pointing. Scores more were approaching across the car park.

A hospital porter – the man the Doctor and Clara had met pushing a wheelchair when they had first arrived – reached out to the Doctor with his free hand. 'I take things,' he said. 'From the patients who don't understand where they are. I steal from them. It's all in my locker. Help me and I'll give it all back. I'll find everyone I stole from and return their belongings.'

'I'll go to church every Sunday,' called a woman from near the back of the group. 'Please help me. I promise!'

'My wife,' said a man to the Doctor's left. 'I'll be faithful to her, I swear. From this moment on. Just get this thing away from me!'

Clara looked from one desperate person to the next. 'What are they doing?' she asked.

'Bargaining,' replied the Doctor. 'It's the next stage of their grief. The next course of the meal for the Shroud.' He checked his watch. 'Just over three hours before the infestation reaches everyone on the planet.' He climbed the steps and addressed the gathering. 'I will help you all,' he promised. 'But I have to ask you to take a step back so we can continue with our work.'

The Shroud victims began to shuffle away, taking their parasites with them. They re-gathered at the edge of the car park and kept a close eye on the Doctor and his friends.

'What can we do?' said Wobblebottom. 'There are

only a hundred of us. We can't treat a whole world in three hours.

'I can help you spread your cheer,' said the Doctor. 'But first, I have jobs for you all. Clowns – get your costumes and props and prepare to get to work.' He spun to face Mae and Warren. 'You two – have you noticed anything odd about the victims of the Shroud?'

'Other than the fact that they're all begging us for help, not much,' said Warren.

'I have,' said Mae. 'They're all adults. We've hardly seen any children.'

'Precisely!' beamed the Doctor. 'Children – mainly – haven't had to endure the same levels of grief that adults have. They haven't lost people who are important to them and, if they have, they've been protected from the very worst feelings. Sadly, there are exceptions – but we're going to have to ignore those for the moment.'

'Why?' asked Warren. 'What do you want us to do?'

'Round up as many children as you can,' said the Doctor. 'Sammy – the young boy we left with Edith Thomas on our way to the newspaper office. Peggy in the police station cells. As many young people as you can find. They'll be scared but, if you can persuade them to join us, they'll swell our numbers considerably. Take the clown car once the props have been unloaded. Fill it with kids!'

'What about me?' asked Clara.

'You and I are heading back to the TARDIS,' said the Doctor. 'But there's just one little thing I have to do first...' He bounded up the few remaining steps and into the hospital reception area, Clara at his heels.

'You again!' exclaimed the guard he'd been stopped by earlier. 'No tricks this time.'

'Wouldn't dream of it,' said the Doctor, whipping out his psychic paper. 'Not when we've got permission from President Lyndon Johnson himself to come inside.'

The soldier took the psychic paper and stared at it in disbelief. 'Access all areas,' he read aloud.

'And all equipment,' said the Doctor, retrieving the paper. 'Which includes your radio.' He held out his hand. 'May I?'

The guard lifted the handset from his radio and passed it to the Doctor, who pressed the talk button and spoke into it. 'Testing, testing, one, two, three... Captain Keating, are you receiving me, over?'

After a second, Keating's voice echoed tinnily through the speaker on the front of the box. 'Doctor? Is that you?'

'It most certainly is,' the Doctor replied. 'How's the General?'

'Sleeping like a baby,' said Captain Keating. 'Was your trip a success?'

'Absolutely!' the Doctor exclaimed. 'And I think I

have a way to make the Shroud release their grip on people, but I'll need some things from you.'

'Just name them.'

'I was hoping you would say that,' said the Doctor with a wink to Clara. 'I'll need all your vehicles – with drivers, a loudspeaker system, and all the pillowcases your men can find.'

There was a brief silence. 'Whatever you say, Doctor. Anything else?'

'There is one other thing...'

Clara smiled to the bemused guard on duty as the Doctor turned away and rattled off another request. 'Don't worry,' she said kindly. 'He has this effect on most people.'

The Doctor spun and tossed the handset back to the guard, then held out his arm for Clara. 'If you would be so kind, Miss Oswald...'

Clara took the Doctor's arm. 'Lead the way!'

Once inside the TARDIS, the Doctor hurried down the steps from the console level and began to root around inside a cupboard. Clara closed the doors and leaned back against them with a sigh.

'What's wrong?' asked the Doctor, not looking up from his search.

'We can't do it, can we?' Clara replied. 'Wobblebottom's right. A hundred Clowns and a handful of children against millions of Shroud. We're vastly outnumbered.'

The Doctor stepped out of the cupboard and

faced her. 'The Shroud focus on negative emotions,' he said. 'We have to be different. Right now, we need to have hope.' He spun back to the cupboard. 'Besides, I just might be able to give the Clowns an advantage.'

He pulled out a large wooden chest and began to rummage through a pile of electrical equipment inside – old kettles, battered TV sets, computer motherboards and more. Every now and again, he would like the look of a piece and set it aside on the floor before going back for more.

'Hope it is, then,' said Clara. 'What can I do to help?'

'Wires,' said the Doctor, pointing to a corridor with a broken desk lamp. 'Down there, fourth turning on the left, second room on the right – you'll find a workroom with lots of wiring hanging from hooks on the wall. Bring me the lot.'

Clara hurried away down the corridor. It looked exactly the same as every other corridor she'd explored during her time on board the TARDIS, and she wondered how the Doctor managed to keep track of them all – especially as he occasionally got lost himself. Only last week, he'd promised her a tour of the aquarium, but had been forced to give up on it after opening doors to the kitchen, the library and two separate rooms filled with what appeared to be boxes of multicoloured scarves.

'Fourth on the left...' She turned into yet another

identical corridor and made for the second door on the right. Swinging it open, she was blasted in the face with a burst of hot steam. She ducked back out into the corridor, allowing the clouds to clear, then peeked back inside. The room was lined with wooden panels, in front of which sat wooden-slatted benches.

'A sauna,' she said to herself, making a mental note to return on a quieter day. She closed the door and tried the next room along, just in case. 'Aha!'

This was the workroom. Tools of all shapes, sizes and materials lay scattered about, or wedged into any number of toolboxes that dotted the floor. There, on the back wall, were coils of wire.

Clara unhooked them, slipping each new coil over her arm to carry it. By the time she was finished, both arms were full and she had several loops of wire draped around her neck. She waddled back to the control room, struggling under the weight.

'At last!' cried the Doctor, jumping up.

Clara made to drop the bundles onto the console, but the Doctor raised a hand to stop her.

'No – don't move. I can see the one I want…' He reached for a roll of thin, bronze wire hooked over her right shoulder and snipped off a piece around six inches in length.

'Perfect!' said the Doctor. 'You can take it back now.'

Clara dumped the rest of the wire on the floor.

'Yeah,' she said. 'That's going to happen.' She circled the console to examine the gadget the Doctor had built from bits of old electronics. 'Is that it?' she asked.

The Doctor slotted the length of wire in place, then held his handiwork up for inspection. It looked like a funnel, with a large opening at one end, and a much narrower hole at the end of a section of pipe at the other. 'Good, eh?'

'What does it do?' Clara asked.

'Well, it amplifies emotions,' said the Doctor. 'Happiness goes in here…' He gestured to the smaller hole. 'And comes out here much, much stronger.'

'The Clowns can use it to treat more people at the same time,' cried Clara.

'Exactly,' said the Doctor. 'I just need to find a couple of screws to hold this pipe on. Can't have it falling off.' He scurried around the central console, examining each piece of equipment. 'These are the right size,' he said, pressing his face down beside the keyboard. 'Could you nip back to the workroom and fetch me a screwdriver?'

Clara folded her arms. 'A screwdriver? Are you serious?'

'Yes,' said the Doctor. 'I need to take the screws out of here and— Oh!' Slowly, he reached inside his jacket and pulled out his sonic. 'Do you know, I don't think I've ever used this for actually removing screws before…'

A few bursts of sonic energy later, the Doctor was able to lift the keyboard off the console. 'Goodness!' he exclaimed, looking at what was underneath as he started to screw the pipe in place on his gadget. 'I wondered where that had got to.'

'What is it?' asked Clara, looking round the Doctor's arm. On the console, underneath where the keyboard had been, was a small square box with two switches at the top. Above it, in what appeared to be felt-tip pen, was written 'Fast Return'.

'The Fast Return switch,' said the Doctor, whirring screws into the pipework with his sonic. 'Think of it like a rewind button for the TARDIS. One side deals with time and the other with space. Press them and we'll end up at our previous location, as though we'd been pulled back there by a bungee cord.'

'But why was it hidden by the keyboard?'

'Must have been covered up during my last redesign. I haven't used it for a long time now,' said the Doctor. 'Not since it got stuck and tried to drag me back through the beginning of the universe.'

'I can see how that would be a problem.'

The final screw in place, the Doctor grabbed the pipe at the end of his gadget and checked that it was now secured. 'Ready?' he asked.

Clara grinned. 'Ready!'

The parade was one of the strangest things that

Warren had ever seen. Dozens of military jeeps and armoured vehicles lined the road outside the hospital, their deep green camouflage hastily covered with colourful curtains and bedspreads. Standing in the back of each truck was a Clown or two, ready to perform.

In front of the military machines, the Clown band were warming up their instruments. Flip Flop was with them, holding out a radio handset which fed directly into a huge pair of speakers strapped to the top of a tank. As the musicians played, their song was amplified out in every direction.

Before the musicians, several dozen children waited nervously, bundles of cotton pillowcases bundled under their arms. The Clowns had applied a little face paint to each of the kids, giving them red noses and drawn-on smiles. Despite their nerves, the youngsters giggled at the sight of one another. Mae and Orma stood with them, trying their best to keep spirits up among the group.

And there, at the head of the parade, were Wobblebottom and the Doctor. The Clown was spinning a drum major's baton, while Clara helped the Doctor into a leather harness that allowed him to carry his gadget in front of himself, and angle it either left or right.

'What's it called?' Wobblebottom asked, eyeing the invention with interest.

'I'm not sure yet,' said the Doctor.

'So give it a name,' said Clara.

'Well, it amplifies emotions, so it could be the Emotion Amplifier... No, on second thoughts, forget that. It's a rubbish name.'

'What about the Fun Gun?' said Clara as she fastened the buckle on the second strap.

'No!' cried the Doctor. 'I'm not having anything with "gun" in the name!'

'OK,' said Clara. 'The Happy Slapper!'

The Doctor stared at her. 'Are you insane?'

'You could call it the Fun Flinger,' suggested Wobblebottom.

'Yes, only it doesn't so much fling the fun out of the big end as squirt it out,' said the Doctor. He raised a finger to silence Clara. 'Whatever you're about to say, Miss Oswald, forget it!'

Clara shrugged. 'Whatever you call it, we can still only use it on one group of people at a time, can't we?'

The Doctor grinned, his eyes sparkling. 'This is the best bit,' he said. 'This is the bit where you get to call me a genius! Because of the tragic events here yesterday, Dallas is filled with television crews from all over the world. I asked Captain Keating to send someone out to tell them all about this, and here they come now...'

Clara heard the sound of engines and looked up to see dozens of vans and trucks approaching, each one painted with the logo of their news team or TV station. Many of them had antennae bobbing about on top as they drove.

'But haven't they been affected by the Shroud?' asked Clara.

The Doctor tried not to look smug, but didn't exactly pull it off. 'TV reporters,' he said. 'Camera and sound operators, technicians, producers – all of them hardened against the less savoury side of the news, just like Mae.'

'So they can hold off the Shroud!' cried Clara, clapping her hands. 'OK, I'll give it to you this once – you're a genius.'

The Doctor raised a finger. 'I'm not done yet…' He smiled. 'They'll broadcast the concentrated joy produced by…' he hoisted up his gadget, '…whatever this thing is called to every country on the planet, severing links with the Shroud worldwide.'

'Even back at home?' asked Clara.

'Well, that looks like a BBC van to me,' said the Doctor, standing on tiptoe to see over the gathering gaggle of reporters. He checked his watch. 'So back in Britain, it's just about teatime on Saturday 23 November 1963 – and the fun is about to start!'

The Doctor turned to survey the waiting procession. 'All right, everyone!' he called out. 'Drivers, follow my lead. Kids, ready with the pillowcases. And Clowns, just like you did back on Semtis – once more with feeling!' He turned back to Wobblebottom with a smile. 'That's it! I'll call this thing the Once More With Feeling.'

'Then let's give it a go,' smiled the Clown. He blew his whistle, and he and the Doctor set off at a march. Behind them, the musicians began to play, the children skipped along to the beat and the military vehicles set off at a crawl. On the back of each truck, the Clowns started to perform. They tumbled, danced and juggled, and twisted long balloons into the shapes of dogs, birds and more.

Warren watched from the steps of the hospital as the parade began. Despite the trouble the world was in, he couldn't help but smile at the spectacle. It was one of the happiest groups of people he had ever seen gathered together in one place. Slowly, the procession snaked its way out of the car park and past the waiting Shroud victims on the sidewalk beyond.

As the Doctor approached the first group of people – each still holding hands with a woman in a blue dress, he spun the Once More With Feeling to face them and pressed a button on the side of the gizmo. There was a whoosh, and a jet of compressed happiness blasted out of the funnel, ruffling the victims' hair. The porter from the hospital was there, and he chuckled.

'Now!' called the Doctor over his shoulder. Mae grabbed a pillowcase from one of the children – a boy named Arran – and dashed over to the porter. In one quick move, she pulled the pillowcase over the head of the Shroud holding his hand, obscuring her face from the man. He laughed again as another burst of happiness hit him and – with a piercing shriek – the Shroud beside him vanished in a shower of blue sparks. The porter stumbled backwards, where one of Captain Keating's soldiers was waiting to catch him.

'It works!' cried Wobblebottom, tossing his baton in the air and waving to urge more fun out of the Clowns.

The Doctor grinned as the porter was helped back towards the hospital by the soldier. 'The Shroud's veils are semi-transparent,' he explained. 'Those affected can see their loved one's eyes through the material – but not when we cover them with a pillowcase. It breaks the mental link – just like it did with Mae when we bandaged her wound. With any luck, unaffected people all over the world will be copying us.'

Slowly, one by one, the victims of the Shroud smiled, giggled and guffawed. With each laugh, Clara, Mae or Orma slid a pillowcase over a Shroud's head, obscuring their features from view. Scream after scream rang out as the aliens exploded into shimmering sapphire particles.

Crowds gathered at the sides of the road, people calling out to the Doctor to aim the Once More With Feeling in their direction and free them from the creature holding their hands. Further back in the group, Mae couldn't help but notice the similarities between this parade and the one she had witnessed the day before that had started all of this.

The Doctor swung the Once More With Feeling to his left, showering the people on the other side of the road with compressed joy. Among them was Dr Ellison, who sniggered happily as the merriment hit her. Orma hid her father's features from view with a pillowcase, and the doctor staggered into the arms of a waiting serviceman. 'Thank you!' she called to the Doctor as he marched past.

'We'd better pick up the pace,' said the Doctor to Wobblebottom. 'We've got a lot of ground to cover, and we haven't got much time before—' He suddenly stopped, Wobblebottom bumping into him.

'What's the matter?' asked the Clown.

'Look at the people,' said the Doctor, shrugging out of his harness and dashing over to the sidewalk.

Wobblebottom blew his whistle to stop the procession as the Doctor studied the people around them. Every single one of the Shroud's victims there had stopped calling out and had dropped their heads to stare at the ground. The musicians halted their song, casting an eerie silence over the area.

'What's happened to them?' asked Clara, hurrying to the Doctor's side.

'They've advanced to the next stage of grief,' said the Doctor, scanning a woman in a smart business suit with his sonic screwdriver. 'The Shroud has increased its rate of feeding, sending their victims into a state of depression. After this, they'll accept their fate and then there's no going back.'

'But it happened to everyone at exactly the same moment,' said Clara, stepping off the pavement to stare further down the street. 'How can that be?'

'I don't know,' said the Doctor, scanning another victim, and then another. 'A hive mind? We already know they possess considerable psychic powers, so maybe…' He checked the readings on his sonic.

'Oh no,' he said quietly.

'What is it?' asked Clara.

'I'm so stupid,' said the Doctor, slapping his palm to his forehead. 'How can I not have seen this?'

'Seen what, Doctor?' Clara demanded. 'What's going on?'

The Doctor turned to face her, his eyes wide with fear. 'The Shroud isn't an alien race,' he said. 'It's one single creature.'

Chapter 14

The Doctor stood with his back to the rest of the group, staring out of the window in Dr Ellison's office. Outside, Flip Flop was leading the other Clowns in the packing away of their equipment.

'I still don't really understand what you mean,' said Mae. 'How can the Shroud be one creature? There are thousands of them. Millions.'

'They're the Shroud's tentacles,' said the Doctor. 'The actual being is the tunnel we passed through to get to Semtis and back. It's a living wormhole with millions of feelers at each end.'

Clara's eyes grew wide. 'But that means, we drove through its stomach. Twice! And those bodies we found embedded in the tunnel walls – it was still digesting them.'

'And worse, I'm afraid,' said the Doctor. 'The appearance of the Shroud in this world looks human – it even scanned as human.'

'You mean the women in the blue veils?' asked Clara.

The Doctor nodded. 'The Shroud is using people it has already fed on like human puppets at the ends of its tentacles.'

'The mental tentacles?' asked Mae.

'It appears they can be real tentacles as well,' said the Doctor. 'If I'm right, the Shroud keeps hold of the last person each of its tentacles attacked, then uses that body to push through into part of its next world.'

'But we knew the people whose faces we saw,' Clara pointed out.

The Doctor sighed heavily. 'The Shroud must alter the basic DNA somehow to match the faces it found in our memories. It still doesn't alter the fact that it broke into this world using what was left of real people.'

'I think I'm going to be sick,' groaned Mae.

'But that must mean the Shroud is a vast being?' said Warren. 'It stretched all the way from one galaxy to another.'

'We drove through its entire length,' said the Doctor. 'Like a standard wormhole, it has the ability to bend time and space, allowing it to reach out over great distances.'

'So it stretched out from Semtis to Earth, and began to feed with the other end?' said Wobblebottom.

'Exactly,' said the Doctor. 'And after it's finished here on Earth, it will release Semtis and seek out another food source from there. My guess is that it needs to stay attached to a planet at either end to anchor itself in space and time while it feeds.'

'But surely this gives us an advantage,' said Clara. 'Instead of fighting off millions of individual aliens, we're only up against a single one.'

'One that's several miles long and can warp the universe to suit itself,' Warren pointed out.

The Doctor picked up the Once More With Feeling and began to buckle himself back into the harness. 'Clara's right,' he said. 'One creature is easier to fight than a million – but now the fight is down to me.'

The Doctor stood at the top of the hospital steps, the Once More With Feeling strapped to his chest. At the opposite end of the car park stood thousands of people and their Shroud counterparts. The group stretched down the street in both directions, every single human with their heads down in silence.

'You know what to do?' the Doctor asked, pulling out his sonic screwdriver and making a few small adjustments to the machine in front of him.

'Yes,' said Clara, reaching out to squeeze the Doctor's arm. 'I'm just worried about you.'

The Doctor flashed her a smile. 'No need to worry about me. This will be as easy as falling off a mushroom on Mechanus.' He winked. 'See you on the other side…'

As Clara hurried away, the Doctor took a deep breath and allowed the Once More With Feeling gadget to reach deep inside his own memories.

Flash!

He was still on Earth, but now in the 22nd century. He wrapped an arm around his granddaughter, Susan, and gave her a hug. 'I er… I erm… I think I must check up on the ship,' he said, shuffling back towards the TARDIS.

'Will you be long?' asked Susan, but the Doctor didn't reply. He watched as his granddaughter walked over to David Campbell, the freedom fighter she had met while battling the Daleks, then hurried inside. He waited until Ian and Barbara had returned, then he finally made his decision and locked the TARDIS doors.

'Grandfather!' screamed Susan, running over to the TARDIS.

'Listen, Susan, please. During all the years I've been taking care of you, you in return have been taking care of me.'

'Grandfather, I belong with you!' Susan cried.

'Not any longer, Susan,' the Doctor responded.

Flash!

Susan! The Doctor felt tears in his eyes. How he

missed her. He looked up to see that several of the blue-veiled women had released their human victims and were crossing the hospital car park towards him. He was clearly a more satisfying-looking meal now that his grief was being amplified. Clara, Mae and Warren were helping the freed people to limp away.

Flash!

'There is no escape, Doctor. Say goodbye to your friends.'

'There must be something we can do!' cried Zoe.

'No,' sighed the Doctor. 'Not this time.' With a heavy heart, he turned to the kilted figure of Jamie McCrimmon. 'Well, goodbye, Jamie.'

'But Doctor, surely…'

The Doctor shook his head. There was nothing he could do. The Time Lords had made their decision. 'Goodbye, Jamie.'

Jamie took the Doctor's hand – his friend's hand – and shook it. 'I won't forget you, you know.'

'I won't forget you,' said the Doctor. 'Now, don't go blundering into too much trouble, will you?'

Despite his feelings, Jamie smiled. 'You're a fine one to talk!'

Slowly, the Doctor turned to his other companion. 'Goodbye, Zoe.'

Flash!

Dozens of blue-veiled women stood at the foot of the hospital steps, staring up at the Doctor.

Flash!

Champagne corks popped for two, very different, reasons. Not only was Jo Grant engaged to be married to Clifford Jones, but the Wholeweal environmental commune had been upgraded to a priority one research complex.

'You got on to your uncle at the United Nations, didn't you?' said the Doctor.

Jo blushed. 'It's only the second time I've ever asked him for anything.'

'Yes. And look where the first time got you.'

'You don't mind, do you?' asked Jo.

'Mind?' asked the Doctor with a smile. 'We might even be able to turn you into a scientist.'

As Brigadier Lethbridge-Stewart made a toast, the Doctor downed his champagne and left Wholeweal for the last time. He climbed into Bessie and, with a final glance back at the cottage, started the engine and drove away into the night.

Flash!

The Doctor was now surrounded by the Shroud, and more women were swarming towards the hospital, their veils blowing in the early evening breeze.

Slowly, he began to back down the corridor behind him.

Flash!

He was in the secondary control room. Sarah Jane Smith entered, carrying a bag and a pot plant. She kicked the door shut behind her. 'A-hem!'

The Doctor wiped his brow, unable to look at her.
'I've had the call from Gallifrey.'

'So...?'

'So I can't take you with me. You've got to go.'

Flash!

The corridor was packed with women in blue veils, all of them advancing on the Doctor as he retreated further into the hospital. He stepped over the large, heavy chain and continued backwards.

Flash!

The Doctor raced back to the controls, spinning dials and pulling levers. 'Please hurry, Doctor!' begged Nyssa. 'We must get Adric off the freighter.'

'The console's damaged!' cried the Doctor.

Tegan stared up at the monitor, a look of horror in her eyes. 'Look!'

'Adric!' yelled Nyssa.

But there was nothing any of them could do but watch as the freighter collided with prehistoric Earth.

Flash!

The streets of Dallas and far beyond were empty of the Shroud. Every single tentacle was reaching into Parkland Memorial Hospital and into the Doctor's mind.

Flash!

The Doctor stared up at the screen in horror, all thoughts of the unfairness of his trial forgotten. He watched as the warrior king, Yrcanos burst into the medical chamber to face a shaven-headed Peri – only that wasn't really Peri any more. Her mind had been swapped with that of the Mentor, Lord Kiv.

Yrcanos roared with rage and triggered the explosion that would kill them both.

Flash!

'I suppose it's time I should be going,' said Mel.

The Doctor looked up from the console. 'Oh…'

'Time that I left…'

Flash!

Fireworks exploded above them to welcome the new millennium.

'Come with me,' said the Doctor.

Grace shook her head. 'I'm gonna miss you.'

'How can you miss me?' exclaimed the Doctor. 'I'm easy to find. I'm the guy with two hearts, remember?'

'That's not what I meant…'

Flash!

Captain Jack Harkness kissed Rose goodbye. 'Wish I'd never met you, Doctor,' he said, his voice trembling slightly with the fear of what was to come. 'I was much better off as a coward.'

The trio shared a final look.

'See you in Hell!' said Jack, then he was gone.

Flash!

Astrid turned to look at the Doctor one last time.

'No!' he begged. But she knew there was no other way out.

Raising the forks, she lifted Max Capricorn's life-support unit clear off the ground and drove for the guard rail surrounding the gantry above the engines.

'*Astrid!*' cried the Doctor as the forklift disappeared over the edge. He pulled his arms away from the Host and ran to the edge in time to see Astrid reaching back up towards him as she plummeted into the flames below.

Flash!

'Doctor!'

The Doctor raced out of the TARDIS at Amy's cry, River Song at his heels.

Rory had vanished, sent back in time by a lone, dying Angel – and now Amy was walking towards the creature.

'Amy, what are you doing?' the Doctor asked, nervously.

'That gravestone – Rory's – there's room for one more name, isn't there?'

The Doctor couldn't believe what he was hearing. 'What are you talking about?' he demanded. 'Come back to the TARDIS, we'll figure something out.'

He grabbed Amy's hand, but she shook him off.

'The Angel, will it send me back to the same time? To him?'

'I don't know,' the Doctor admitted. 'Nobody knows!'

'But it's my best shot, yeah?'

'No!'

'Doctor, shut up!' cried River. 'Yes, yes it is!'

'Well then,' said Amy. 'I just have to blink, right?'

'No!' begged the Doctor.

'It'll be fine,' Amy said, trying to reassure him. 'I know it will. I'll… I'll be with him, like I should be. Me and Rory together.'

She clutched River's hand, making her promise to look after the Doctor, trying hard to ignore his final protests.

'Raggedy man,' she said, spinning to face her best friend. She looked into his eyes one last time. 'Goodbye.'

Flash!

The Doctor's tears were flowing freely now, his back pressed against the open doorway of the TARDIS. He could feel the Shroud's tentacles inside his mind, feeding off his grief, and the food was plentiful.

And it was time for one last push. Time for him to relive a fresh memory. Time for him to visit one final place in his mind. One he'd been avoiding all these months.

The Doctor closed his eyes.

Flash!

He was standing near the gates of a different graveyard, the gentle summer breeze ruffling his thick hair and pulling at the edges of his bow tie. A few hundred yards ahead, a large crowd gathered together – a mixture of civilians and UNIT personnel.

A man in uniform stepped up to place a folded flag on the polished surface of an oak coffin. Like almost everyone else there, he had aged since the Doctor had last seen him.

John Benton saluted the coffin, then turned to the UNIT soldiers standing beside the grave. 'Rifle party!' he commanded. 'Five rounds rapid.'

Crack! The first volley sent a flock of birds flapping up into the air. A man in a crumpled suit rested on the question mark handle of his umbrella and watched them disappear.

Crack! Liz Shaw buried her face against the shoulder of a man in a velvet jacket and an opera cape.

Crack! Mike Yates exchanged a sad glance with a small, tousled-haired fellow in an over-sized fur coat.

Crack! A man in a coat of rainbow colours wrapped an arm around Jo Grant.

Crack! A short-haired man lowered his head and pushed his hands into the pockets of his leather jacket.

Slowly, the coffin lowered into its final resting place.

Flash!

Several years had passed, and leaves now tumbled from the branches hanging over the cemetery. The mourners and their extravagant floral tributes were long gone. In their place, standing to attention on either side of the marble headstone, were bunches of flowers in more permanent glazed pots.

The rain pattered down, leaving the ground slippery and soft underfoot. Eventually, the Doctor came out from the shelter of the trees.

He slowly approached the grave, raindrops dripping from his hair and down his cheeks. He stood and read the name carved into the marble: Brigadier Alistair Gordon Lethbridge-Stewart.

Quietly, he saluted.

Flash!

The Doctor tumbled back through the doorway of the TARDIS.

Mae dashed to kneel beside him. 'Ready?' she asked as she unbuckled the harness holding the Once More With Feeling in place. On the other side of the doorway, the corridor was filled with blue-veiled women, their hands outstretched.

The Doctor clamped his hands to the sides of his head, his fingers clawing through his hair as if trying to get to the millions of mouths as they feasted on his mind. His eyes met with Mae's and he managed to nod.

'This is the TARDIS!' said Warren into his radio handset. 'The Doctor is in. You are cleared to go!'

Outside in the car park, Wobblebottom checked that the clamp at the end of the long chain was firmly attached to the rear bumper of the clown car, then he jumped into the passenger seat and gave Flip Flop the signal. 'Understood, TARDIS,' he replied into his own radio. 'Starting stage two now.'

Flip Flop stomped onto the accelerator pedal and drove the clown car headlong towards the hospital wall. The entrance to the living wormhole shimmered as the car plunged through and into the belly of the Shroud. Once inside, the Clowns leapt from the car, unhooked the chain and plunged its hook hard into the rough stone of the tunnel, hammering it down to ensure it stayed embedded in the rock.

'Stage two completed!' cried Wobblebottom into the radio.

Inside the TARDIS, Warren received the message and turned to give Clara the thumbs up as she waited at the console. She smiled, then slammed her hand down onto the Fast Return switch.

Chapter 15

The engines wheezed as the TARDIS leapt into the air and reversed back towards the Vortex. The metal links in the big, thick chain creaked in protest as it began to take the full weight of what was connected to the other end.

'I don't understand,' said Mae. 'I thought this ship couldn't take off while the end of the wormhole was wrapped around the world.'

The Doctor slumped into the seat beside the stairs. 'We're not taking off,' he said. 'We're rewinding to the TARDIS's last point in space and time – the planet Venofax.' He gripped his head with his hands. 'And we'd better hurry up in getting there, because I'm losing memories by the second. If this goes on for much longer, I might forget how to dress so cool.'

Clara opened her mouth to comment, but thought better of it.

Suddenly, the TARDIS jolted and a terrifying screech rang out, setting everyone's teeth on edge. The Doctor pulled himself to his feet and crossed to the console, hanging on to the monitor. 'We've done it,' he said. 'We've detached the end of the Shroud from Earth. No, wait. Detached isn't right – it sounds too... detached. Ripped? No. Unsuckered! We've unsuckered the Shroud from the Earth!'

Warren stood near to the open doors, watching the planet fall away below him. 'Whatever you call it, what about the people down there, Doctor?' he said. 'Are they safe?'

The Doctor nodded. 'The Shroud released them all to feed on me,' he said. 'Although some of the tentacles have just detached themselves from my mind.' He ran his fingers through his hair, as if trying to locate them by touch alone. 'And I think I know where they've gone...'

Inside the wormhole, thirty Clowns clung on to the other end of the chain, holding it down and ensuring the hook at the end didn't pull free from the rock. Ahead of them, the shimmering portal began to evaporate, allowing them to see out to the blackness of space beyond.

And then the tentacles began to snake inside.

These weren't invisible 'mental tentacles' like the

Doctor had described, but physical tendrils of flesh, purple in colour and covered with oozing suckers.

'OK!' cried Wobblebottom. 'Here we go. This is what the Doctor warned us might happen…'

The tentacles attacked, lashing out at the Clowns and trying to wrap around them. The Clowns fought back, grabbing polished swords from their props cases – swords more used to plunging through wooden caskets with glamorous assistants inside than battle – but they did the job.

Orma lopped off the end of one of the tentacles as it came for her. The severed tip dropped at her feet and writhed on the ground, leaking a viscous pink fluid. Closing her eyes, the Clown raised her foot and stomped on it.

Flip Flop was clutching a saw he'd last used to pretend to cut someone in half. He swung the serrated edge out at the nearest purple appendage, cutting deep into its flesh. The tunnel around them echoed with a horrible scream. Then another tentacle whipped over his head and quickly wrapped itself around Flip Flop's throat. Before anyone could come to his rescue, the Clown was lifted off his feet, spun round in the air, and catapulted through the end of the tunnel and out into the blackness beyond.

Wobblebottom roared with rage and called for a fellow Clown to toss him a fire stick and bottle of fuel. Taking a big mouthful of the fluid, he spat through the flame, expelling a vast cloud of fire that enveloped the guilty tentacle, burning it to a crisp in a matter of seconds.

Briefly, the purple tendrils retreated, waving in the air near the tunnel mouth. The Clowns took the opportunity to rearm themselves.

Wobblebottom cricked his neck from side to side. 'You're going down,' he snarled to the writhing tentacles. 'You're going down to Clown Town!'

'There!' said the Doctor, pressing his fingertips to his throbbing forehead and gesturing to the monitor with the other hand. 'There's Venofax!'

'And what do we do when we get there?' asked Warren.

'Give me that sock again,' said the Doctor.

'I threw it in the garbage,' Warren reminded him.

'Then give me the other one.'

A moment later, the foot had been snipped from the end of Warren's second sock. The Doctor took the nectarine proffered by Clara and slipped it into one end of the sock tunnel, just like before – only this time, he looped the other end round in a circle and slipped that over the nectarine as well.

'It's like a time loop, or a space loop,' said the Doctor. 'Only a worm loop.'

'You mean you're going to keep the Shroud trapped there for ever?' asked Mae.

'I promised to find it another planet,' said the Doctor. 'I didn't say anything about letting it leave.'

Bong!

'The Cloister Bell!' announced the Doctor. 'We're back to our last destination...'

The TARDIS began to shake violently from side to side, forcing everyone to cling to the console to avoid been thrown to the ground.

'... and I think the Shroud has just figured out what we're planning to do with it.'

'How?' asked Clara.

'Hello,' said the Doctor, with a smile. 'Millions of mental tentacles squirming around in my head. I guess it found the folder marked "Devious Plans".'

This time, the TARDIS shook so hard that Warren and Mae did lose their balance.

'Blimey!' said the Doctor in amazement. 'Look at that!'

He ran to the doorway. Outside, a three-mile-long worm was twisting and curling madly, like an eel trying desperately to free itself from a fisherman's hook. Below, the emerald sea bubbled and frothed over the surface of the planet.

Clara joined him to watch the spectacle. 'It doesn't look happy,' she commented.

'I wouldn't be either, most likely,' said the Doctor. 'Not if all I was going to get to eat for the rest of my life was a soapy avocado smoothie. However, it's worth remembering that avocado is incredibly good at boosting your serotonin levels. It's a natural anti-depressant.'

A smile spread across Clara's face. 'You're going to feed liquid anti-depressant to a furious living wormhole that feeds on negative emotions?'

The Doctor winked. 'Good, aren't I?'

Clara was forced to grip the doorframe for support as the TARDIS lurched again. 'Not unless we can find a way to get that thing down there to swallow the planet,' she cried. 'I doubt it will do it voluntarily.'

'I've got that covered as well,' beamed the Doctor. He spun and aimed a blast from his sonic screwdriver at the microphone switch on the console. 'Hello again, Penny!' he cried.

'Doctor!' replied the voice of Professor Penelope Holroyde. 'Is everything OK?'

'Yes,' said the Doctor. 'Well, no. Well, sort of. Bit difficult to explain, really. Listen – I know you only left us a few minutes ago from your point of view, but have you managed to start that second engine yet?'

'Just now,' said Professor Holroyde. 'We're running on full power again.'

'Good,' said the Doctor. 'Then I wonder if you'd mind turning round and coming back to give us a hand with something...'

A few moments later, the radio crackled into life once again as the SS *Howard Carter* came into view. 'What in the name of sanity is that?'

'It's called the Shroud,' said the Doctor, racing

back up to the console and grabbing the radio handset. 'And it's been a very naughty… er, worm. Now, can you grab the free end with your front pincers and drag it down and over the planet below?'

'I should think we could manage that,' said Penny.

'Excellent!' beamed the Doctor. 'I'm just going to put you on hold while I check in with my other team. Doctor out.' He held a hand over the microphone and grinned. 'I've got two teams!'

Clara wagged a finger. 'Don't get cocky.'

The Doctor pulled a serious face and raised the radio again. 'Come in, Wobblebottom,' he cried. 'How are you all doing down there?'

There was a hiss, and then the sounds of an ongoing battle emerged from the TARDIS speakers. 'We're holding steady,' Wobblebottom replied. 'But it's not easy. 'We're fighting a lot of tentacles here.'

'There are going to be a lot more of them very soon,' the Doctor warned. 'But you know what to do with them.'

'We do indeed!'

'Good man!' exclaimed the Doctor. 'Doctor out.' He spun on the spot, then raced back to the doorway to look out. In the distance, he could just make out the SS *Howard Carter* being buffeted around at the far end of the Shroud. 'Penny! Talk to me…'

'We've locked on, Doctor,' said Penny. 'But it's trying to shake us off!'

'Don't worry,' said the Doctor, turning and running back up to the TARDIS controls. 'I'll be with you very soon.' He tossed the radio to Warren, then adjusted a number of dials and switches. 'Now then, sexy,' he crooned to the time rotor. 'How about a quick spin around that little planet down there?'

Then he slammed the flight lever down.

The Shroud screeched as the TARDIS fell fast, looping around the far side of the dwarf planet, but the noise was soon dulled as the body of the worm splashed down into the frothy green sea.

'It's going to be a bit of a stretch,' cried the Doctor as the TARDIS swooped over the top of the waves. The chain was pulling taut, and their movement slowing as they neared the other end of the Shroud, held just above the water by Penny and her team.

'Well, the Shroud could do with going on a diet,' said Mae with a smile.

The Doctor grabbed the radio again. 'OK, Wobblebottom – here come the rest of the tentacles…' Then he closed his eyes and pushed the Shroud's feelers from his mind.

Inside the Shroud, the Clowns watched as the two ends of the tunnel were dragged closer and closer together.

The openings suddenly erupted in a seething mass of new tentacles and, at the sight of these, Wobblebottom and his team dropped their weapons.

Working quickly, each Clown grabbed two tentacles – one from each end of the wormhole – and began to twist them together, just like they did with modelling balloons in their therapy sessions back home.

'I don't want anything fancy,' Wobblebottom ordered. 'No poodles or giraffes – just good, solid lock twists! This thing has to hold together for a very long time.'

The Clowns' white gloves were a blur. They twisted the tentacles together as quickly as they could, the rubbery flesh squeaking and protesting, just like genuine balloons.

'Has anyone else noticed the sea?' asked Orma, dumping one pair of tentacles and quickly grabbing another.

Wobblebottom looked down to find green, soapy water washing around his oversized shoes. 'Don't worry,' he said. 'The Doctor promised to get us out of here.'

Outside, there was a splash as the far end of the chain was released and dropped into the water. Wobblebottom turned to two burly Clowns on the other side of the car. 'With me.'

The three of them leapt over the gap from one end of the wormhole to the other. Together they hauled the heavy chain out of the sea and hammered the free end deep into the inner skin of the Shroud. 'Just in case some of the knots don't hold in the tentacles,' the Clown explained.

As they re-joined their red-nosed colleagues, the tunnel began to vibrate and echo with a wheezing rasp – like a circus elephant with a bad chest. Slowly, a blue box pulsed into view.

A door opened, and the figure silhouetted in the light shining from behind reached up to adjust its bow tie.

'Anybody fancy a lift?'

The TARDIS materialised next to the stage in the underground theatre.

Wobblebottom opened the door and stepped out to be greeted by his friends. 'He did it!' he called back into the ship. 'We're back on Semtis!'

The other door was flung open and the clown car puttered out, just about making it through the gap. It parked up beside a colourful tepee and a long line of Clowns began to climb out.

The Doctor, Clara, Mae and Warren joined Wobblebottom outside the TARDIS.

'I'm so sorry about Flip Flop,' said the Doctor, shaking the Clown's hand.

Wobblebottom smiled, tears running down his cheeks and smudging his make-up. 'He was a brave man, and a good Clown,' he said.

Music began to play. The group looked up as another Wanter was led onto the stage and a therapy session got under way.

'Flip Flop was the one who insisted we try to help

people who had been attacked by the Shroud,' said Wobblebottom.

'And he did it,' said the Doctor. 'He helped countless people here, and billions on Earth. You should never forget him.'

Wobblebottom smiled. 'We won't.'

Mae and Clara said their goodbyes to the Clowns, then the Doctor turned back to the TARDIS doors. 'Come on, gang,' he said, sniggering to himself at the word. 'Gang!'

'I think I'm going to stay,' said Warren.

The Doctor raised an eyebrow. 'Really?'

Warren pulled a coin from his pocket and made to toss it, then instead he simply handed it to the Doctor. 'I'm certain,' he said. 'There's a lot of work to be done here, and I think I can help.'

'It's your decision,' said the Doctor. 'Oh, and I think you'd really make good use of this...' He reached inside the doorway of the TARDIS and grabbed the Once More With Feeling.

'Thank you, Doctor,' said Warren. He looked up as Orma came to stand beside him and take his hand in hers.

'That works so much better when two humans do it,' commented the Doctor. Then, with a final glance around, he led Mae and Clara back into the TARDIS and closed the doors.

Warren, Wobblebottom and the other Clowns watched as the blue box faded away, engines rasping.

'We'll need to think of a new name for you,' said Wobblebottom. 'Warren Skeet is OK, but it's not going to raise any smiles when folk hear it.'

Warren shrugged. 'The kids at school always called me Skeeter...'

Wobblebottom grinned. 'Perfect!'

Chapter 16

General Harley B. West sat up with a gasp. He was out of uniform and in bed – but this wasn't his own bed. He was in a hospital ward.

'Nurse!' he cried out. 'Nurse!'

A figure moved in the chair next to the bed, waking up from a deep sleep. It was Captain Keating.

'Keating!' spat the General. 'What's the meaning of this?'

'Don't get up,' cried Keating, helping the General to lie down again. 'The doctor says you have to get as much rest as you can.'

The General frowned. 'Really?'

'Certainly,' said Captain Keating. 'Especially after all the hard work you did ridding the country of those faces.'

'They're gone?'

'All thanks to you, sir,' said Keating. 'Wait here – I think I can hear the doctor outside.' He hurried out through the ward door.

General West slumped back against his pillows. He'd gotten rid of the faces himself? An entire Russian attack repelled by his hand? Then why couldn't he remember any of it? He had to get back to his office and read up on the paperwork. Pulling back the covers, he swung his legs off the bed.

'General West!' cried a female voice. 'What do you think you're doing?' Dr Mairi Ellison strode up to the bed, a fierce expression etched across her features.

The General froze at the commanding tone. 'I have to go back to work, madam,' he said.

'Madam?' exclaimed the doctor. 'Don't you "madam" me! I am your medical consultant, and you are under strict instructions not to move from that bed for at least another two days!'

'Two days?' the General rumbled. 'I can't lie here for two days! I've got work to do.'

'Actually, sir – you haven't,' said Captain Keating.

'What on earth are you talking about, Keating?'

Dr Ellison turned to Keating. 'This is what I was referring to,' she said. 'Loss of memory as a result of the chemical attack.'

The General's cheeks flushed. 'Chemical attack? What chemical attack?'

'The, er… chemical attack the faces launched just before you blasted them off the face of the planet, sir,' said Keating.

'Oh yes,' muttered General West to himself. 'That chemical attack. Of course.'

Dr Ellison collected the chart from the end of the General's bed and began to make some notes. The General watched her carefully, his mind racing.

'Do you know, Keating,' he said eventually. 'I think I deserve a holiday after saving the day like that. And I do remember saving the day quite clearly.'

'I doubt anyone in Washington would deny you a period of leave, sir,' said Captain Keating. 'In fact, there was mention of this battle being the highlight of your career. And that, if you were to retire now, there could even be a parade of some description in your honour.'

'A parade, you say?' said the General, lifting his head up. 'With ticker tape, do you think?'

'I would say there would almost certainly be ticker tape, sir.'

General West lay back against his pillows with a smile. Retire? Well, he was certainly due some rest and relaxation after everything he'd just been through. He could go hunting. He'd always wanted to slap on a plaid cap and spend the weekend shooting innocent creatures in the forest. People got so upset when you shot a fellow human being these days – even a Russian – but they positively encouraged you to blast a barrel or two into the side of a stag. And then there was the matter of a ticker tape parade...

'Yes,' he said. 'Maybe I *will* retire...'

'That's wonderful to hear, General!' said Captain Keating with a smile. 'Is there anything I can get you before you change your mind? Coffee, perhaps?'

'Oh, yes,' said the General brightly. 'Coffee would be wonderful.'

Captain Keating joined Dr Ellison at the foot of the bed where the General couldn't see her slip a small vial of sedative into his hand.

'One coffee coming right up, General West.'

22 October 1962

The Doctor and Clara stood in the doorway to the TARDIS and watched as Mae approached her grandmother's bed. The old woman opened her eyes, delighted to find her granddaughter smiling down at her.

'How long does she have?' asked Clara.

'A couple of days,' the Doctor replied.

'And that's why you agreed to break all your rules about travelling back along someone's timeline?'

'Rules are meant to be broken,' said the Doctor. 'Besides, the Mae from this time period is busy with newspaper work in Washington and can't get a flight back. Not now I've temporarily jammed the radar at Dulles International Airport, at least. Who'll know?'

Clara smiled. 'You will.'

'I'll try to cope.'

They stood in silence for a while. Mae and her grandmother were holding hands and laughing together.

'How did you do it?' asked Clara.

The Doctor turned to her. 'How did I do what?'

'Push the Shroud from your mind. There were millions of tentacles in there, all attacking you. How did you free yourself from them so the Clowns could tie them together?'

'The same way I got them in there in the first place,' said the Doctor. 'By thinking of my friends.'

'If your friends mean that much to you, then you're a very lucky man,' said Clara.

'I know,' smiled the Doctor.

'Want to know what this friend is thinking right now?'

'What?' asked the Doctor. 'Is it that you'd like to be taller? Because I think you should be taller. When I hug you, I can feel your breath on my chest. It's weird.'

'No!' exclaimed Clara, giving the Doctor a playful punch on the arm. 'I think you'll find that I'm normal height. It's you that's all lanky and stringy.'

'Stringy?'

'It's like looking at you in one of those fairground mirrors sometimes,' said Clara. She turned and stepped back into the TARDIS. 'No, I'm wondering if there were any more of those giant Shroud things floating around the universe.'

The Doctor smiled to himself, then his eyes grew wide as what Clara had said finally sunk in. He opened his mouth to call Mae back to the TARDIS, then paused. Fishing Warren's coin from his pocket, he flipped it and checked the result.

'Tails,' he said to himself. 'No need to rush.'

30 September 3006

Bev Sanford shuffled forward with the rest of the queue towards the entrance to the President's Deck, trying unsuccessfully to remove the sticky price tag from her bunch of freshblooms™. These things were supposed to peel off easily, but they never did. Now the already cheap plastic wrapped around the artificial stems looked worse than before. The woman in front of her was holding a beautiful bouquet of white roses and lilies. They were real flowers, too. Where the hell had she got those on Station Epsilon? Nowhere legal, that's for sure.

Bev had visited three separate sell-stalls this morning – all of which were sold out of freshblooms™ – before resorting to the last bunch in the bucket outside the android refuelling station. Of course, if

Jeff had bothered to get his lazy butt out of bed, he could have taken her to the hypermarket on the mall level first thing.

She'd only invited him over because she'd not wanted to be alone last night. He hadn't remembered, of course, but it was exactly a year since her mum had finally lost her battle with cancer, and Bev had spent the entire day at work feeling as though she was outside her own body, looking in. Everyone around her seemed to be carrying on with their lives as though it was just another day – which, she accepted, for them it was.

What she needed was a distraction, an evening of fun to take her mind off things. In the end, however, all she got was a cold syntho-meat takeaway (which she had paid for herself), short shrift on the bottle of recycled wine and part way into the second episode of Jeff's *Galaxy's Greatest Pod Crashes* vid-disc before his snoring meant she couldn't hear the view-screen any more.

He was still out of it when she'd turned the radio on for something to pass the time while the coffee autoheated this morning. That's when she'd heard the news. Attackers had breached security during the night and shot President Winza dead. She'd just announced a crackdown on illegal gambling and smuggling on Epsilon, and this was how the scum she wanted off the decks had reacted.

Bev was almost at the front of the queue now.

The woman with the roses had produced a white teddy bear to go with them, and was busy writing a message into a matching 'With Condolences' card. More black-market products, but no one would say anything about them. Not today.

The flowers at the entrance to the President's Deck were already several feet deep and, thankfully, plenty of them looked as though they were last-minute sell-stall purchases. She waited until the roses woman had arranged her tribute, then she bent to add her own flowers to the bunches already there.

She was just about to leave when she spotted the face in the bouquet behind hers. The roses woman's teddy had pressed the flowers down, squashing the petals together so that they looked like... No, it couldn't be!

The face turned to look at her, then it opened its mouth and spoke. 'Beverly!'

Bev stared, her eyes pricking with tears. 'Mum?'

Acknowledgements

Many thanks to Justin Richards for inviting me to write this book, and for my family for putting up with me while I did so. Thanks also to top *Doctor Who* pals Mark Wright and Cavan Scott for their support and encouragement on the days when I felt as though I'd lost the ability to string a sentence together. Special thanks, though, go to Beverly Sanford, who kept an eye on the story as I wrote, making sure it all made some sort of sense.

BBC
DOCTOR WHO

Plague of the Cybermen

JUSTIN RICHARDS

'They like the shadows.'

'What like the shadows?'

'You know them as Plague Warriors...'

When the Doctor arrives in the 19th-century village of
Klimtenburg, he discovers the residents suffering from
some kind of plague – a 'wasting disease'. The victims
face a horrible death – but what's worse, the dead seem
to be leaving their graves. The Plague Warriors have
returned...

The Doctor is confident he knows what's really
happening; he understands where the dead go, and he's
sure the Plague Warriors are just a myth.

But as some of the Doctor's oldest and most terrible
enemies start to awaken, he realises that maybe – just
maybe – he's misjudged the situation.

*A thrilling, all-new adventure featuring the Doctor as
played by Matt Smith in the spectacular hit series from BBC
Television.*

U.S. $9.99 (Canada: $11.99) ISBN: 978-0-385-34676-4

DOCTOR WHO

The Dalek Generation

NICHOLAS BRIGGS

'The Sunlight Worlds offer you a life of comfort and plenty. Apply for your brand new home now, by contacting us at the Dalek Foundation.'

Sunlight 349 is one of countless Dalek Foundation worlds, planets created to house billions of humanoids suffering from economic hardship. The Doctor arrives at Sunlight 349, suspicious of any world where the Daleks are apparently a force for good – and determined to find out the truth.

He soon finds himself in court, facing the 'Dalek Litigator'. But do his arch enemies really have nothing more to threaten than legal action? The Doctor knows they have a far more sinister plan – but how can he convince those who have lived under the benevolence of the Daleks for a generation?

Convince them he must, and soon. For on another Foundation planet, archaeologists have unearthed the most dangerous technology in the universe...

A thrilling, all-new adventure featuring the Doctor as played by Matt Smith in the spectacular hit series from BBC Television.

U.S. $9.99 (Canada: $11.99) ISBN: 978-0-385-34674-0